I0683083

Twisted Torment

Ramblings of a Bipolar Mind

By Julie Williams

1

I dedicated this Book to my beautiful Nanna.

Phyllis Mary Brook.

17th July 1917 – 20th June 2003.

The years have passed by since you left me, my heart still aches. I will never forget you.

Love you forever my BFF.

Acknowledgments.

Book Cover Design by my Daughter Samantha-Laura Williams who is 11 ☺ well done.

Book editing done by my oldest son Nathan.

My Mother - Nola Gentle, my sisters Kylie, Lorraine and Penny who were the inspirations for my book. And of course my Nanna.

My other children - Mathew, Mitchell and Natalie. Future daughter's in-law Michelle and Lauren. Thank you for all your support and endless encouragement.

My Husband Warren and all my beautiful friends for believing in me. To everyone who has bipolar or a mental illness be strong, be proud and love who you are. ☺

Contents

Chapter 1

Melinda

"Get away you filthy child! Go home never come here again!" Screams a woman as she grabs her child and runs inside.

Melinda was left standing out on the footpath not sure what just happened, or was this dream? Her mind is confused, too young to understand, feeling like she woke up in the middle of a nightmare; crying as she walks home. She climbs in an opened window to find her mother still asleep and uncovered. Melinda walks over to open a window as the Room smelt of cheap alcohol and cigarettes. Melinda's mother a pretty woman, she fell pregnant at the age of 18, shortly after marrying Michael Reid, a soldier seven years her senior.

Michael went to fight in World War 2 six weeks before Melinda was born. A daughter he never knew, a father she would never know. The only memory she has of her father was a picture her mother kept next to her bed along with the dreaded army telegram dated eleven years ago. Mable found life hard coping with working to support her and her young child. The loss of her husband so young plagued her health for many years. As Melinda got older Mable became worse. She was drinking and her behaviour was very weird. Some nights Melinda would find her mother cleaning or just crying for no reason, frustrated and losing control over the simplest of things. Melinda recalls one night she found her mother washing walls after midnight, crying uncontrollably because they just didn't seem to be clean in her mind. Mable seemed to slip off into a world of her own, blankly staring at nothing... Leaving Melinda to grow up quickly and take control.

"What do you want to be, when you grow up, my sweetheart?" Asks Mable, as she reaches for a cigarette.

"No Mummy I don't want to grow up, I want to be an angel. I want to help people when they are sad and lost." Melinda runs off to get dinner ready.

"Mel wait, I have something for you." calls Mable as she reaches under her bed then hands Melinda a brown paper bag. It contained a new pair of black boots.

"Thank you so much, are they my size?" asks Melinda - hugging the boots excitedly jumping up and down.

Laughing at her Mable replied. "Go try them on child let's see."

The simple pair of boots took Mable months to save for as her job as a housekeeper was barely enough for rent and food was always basic. It was a job she hated for her employers were very wealthy dairy farmers. Mr Booth, a gentle quiet man ran about doing his daily duties very quietly, never saying more than "Good morning".

Up at 3am daily to run his farm, he worked very long hours, seven days a week.

Mrs Booth however was a different kettle of fish. A showy woman, she loved her fine clothes and shoes. She would run about town with a false attitude often gossiping viscously. "The Dairy Queen" as the locals called her, behind her back.

She wasn't nice to Mable; in fact she was downright nasty! As far as she was concerned Mable was just an employee. So easily, thinking of herself as the better woman - often belittling Mable over the smallest of details, comments that Mable would take to heart and never being able to let go.

One time accusing Mable of eating a piece of bread as Mrs Booth used to count all the food; she wasn't a person who liked to share.

The dairy farm was in far North Queensland where it rained almost 9 months out of 12, the trees were green and the grass was very lush. A dairy farmers dream with a good combination of healthy cows.

There weren't many people living in the actual township. Mainly people lived on the farmland milking their cows for milk and cheese. Lorries came daily to pick up the full cans of lovely warm milk that would be treated, and then sent to the shops to be sold to the consumers in 1 litre glass bottles.

Every morning at 4 am when Mr Booth went for the cows the mist would come over the hills like some scene from a space movie and by the time the cows were milked and being turned back into the paddocks the mist would have been replaced by a constant drizzling rain.

It was a good life, one would think people with that joy in their lives would have a more pleasant and caring attitude of those less fortunate.

Melinda was happy to go back to school; she was now in 6th grade, although she loved her mother dearly, she was glad to be a child at least from 9 to 3. Melinda only had one friend a girl named Phyllis, most of the children at her school called her names and treated her badly.

"Your mother's crazy she is madder than the mad hatter" were taunts she would hear daily. Mothers not allowing their children to play with Melinda, fearing the craziness would spread. But not Phyllis or her family they were different, Phyllis was a lovely sharing child.

Many times when Melinda found herself alone she would go down to the creek and read getting lost in a world far away from hers. She would dream she was a lost princess, trying to find a way out or to simply become invisible - that would be even better.

"Mum, Mum" yelled Melinda running back into the room.

"Look, look, my new boots fit perfectly", spinning around.

Mable looked up at her daughter smiling. "I am sorry I am not a perfect mother. I am so sorry you bear the brunt of people's gossip." Melinda looked puzzled.

"Mum you are perfect and I don't care what anyone thinks as long as we love each other, that is all that matters."

But Mable knew that her moods were affecting them both. Doctors didn't help they had no answers as there wasn't anything physically wrong with her. It was all in her head, but she wasn't crazy or insane. Mable was just lost in a maze with no way out.

Sometimes she was childlike lost reverted, other times she was fiercely independent. Mable's parents had offered her a house and to help her with Melinda. She refused choosing to live in another town raising her daughter on her own.

Chapter 2
Katie

In 1968, a little girl is born with a sad, unhappy soul. Something happened when she was only little, causing confused feelings. I never understood what made me sad. From a very early age, I knew I was different I had pain yet I wasn't in pain.

At age 5, I can still remember a nightmare as if it was only yesterday. I'm screaming and yelling; my Mother was lying on the floor tied up she has been badly beaten. I look down at my feet the bad man had shaved the soles off, with a potato peeler. I don't feel any pain I just look at my bleeding feet. I didn't try to walk because I know it will hurt.

"Now you can't run away can you?" He yells at me waving a knife.

Then I hear the little Girl,

"Wake up Katie. Wake up! It will be alright, just wake up!"

It was just a dream or was it? Life becomes harder as you get older, your mind confused, it becomes hard to remember your childhood. So hard, as the years turned into torment, twisting you out of shape.

Travelling on a plane for what seemed like days to a 5 year old. Getting locked in the toilet on the plane. So upset, crying and banging on the door. Yes very funny now but not back then. Arriving in Singapore, in 1973, was a culture shock. Beggars on the street, market stalls are everywhere. Men pedalling away on bikes, towing chairs on wheels.

I remember buses carrying way too many people. People with a totally different appearance and a language new to me - only a few people were able to speak English. Then to the Army village in Changi, playing in the street with other army kids, hearing rifle shots in the distance. Discovering in later years that the noise was coming from neighbouring 'Changi Prison' - Dad told me that it was Rifle practice when I asked. I later learnt it was Prisoners being executed.

A Yellow Teddy Bear a present given to my mum for me before I was born always around somewhere. The old terrace style house, I remembered it always felt cold even though the weather in Singapore was always hot and humid. Cement walls and tiny tiled pattern floors with a massive dormitory styled room with 6 beds in a line. Huge drains ran around the back yard that I learned were monsoon drains. At the back of the house there was a small free standing room where I spent hours playing on my own, with visions of my dad and neighbours killing rats that dared to venture out of the drains. I remember having to boil water and add pills before we drank it. Waiting for the postman to deliver care packages from my Nannas, which were always full of lollies, books and things, we couldn't get in Singapore.

We started school at 7am to beat the heat and finished at 1pm. We would have a fresh carton of milk at school.

Our Ahma, this word meant maid, hardly spoke any English. I remember an old woman, Kim with multiple missing teeth, in her 50's. Mother of many, she always smiled as she busied herself going about the daily chores. I remember going home with her, a little Aussie child. A home of mainly non-English speaking people. What a wonderful multi-cultural experience! I remember the local ice-cream man, riding a bicycle with a fridge cart. Five cents for an ice-cream. Multiculturalism was alive with people from many nations.

Nightmares again, tormenting my young mind. Always violent with screaming and yelling. Waking up to my mother battered and bruised, constantly wearing sunglasses and long sleeves. I remember my father was a violent aggressive man with an explosive temper, though he never appeared in my nightmares. I learnt from an early to avoid Him as much as I could. Nightmares were making me sad and withdrawn, separating me from the other children. I remember waking up from nightmares, feeling sad with a desperate need to overcome the feeling I was to blame. Some dreams seemed so real, making me feel exhausted and drained. A mind so young unable to handle myself, unable to explain my feelings. Something so simple becomes earth shattering like getting clothes ready for a party, then too scared on the day to wear them. Frightened I might draw too much attention to myself.

Watching black and white movies and drinking salt water hoping to turn into a mermaid. So I could swim away to a life of happiness and be free of the pain.

Returning to Queensland, Australia in the late 70s, I repeated grade 4, never going to 3rd grade. There were wonderful memories of doing grade 4 twice; two classes were combined with 2 innovated teachers, well before their time, creating 2 years of wonderful memories. I found God when I was 10 years joined the Salvation Army. I was a Young Christian Soldier it was a wonderful new found freedom. Memories of playing the tambourine, friendly children and adults, knocking on doors for the Salvation Shield appeal. With nightmares more frequent and terrifying, I woke one morning crying with unexplained pain, feeling like I had sinned. Needing to ask God for forgiveness, even though I had not been bad.

One night after a short time, I was woken to someone knocking on my window. Scared, I remember I never looked. I just ran and told my parents. My Dad went outside to look and found my young friend from S.A.Y.C.S. Megan was 10 years old. I remember her tears and hysterical sobbing. While alone with her in my room, while my parents spoke to the police. I listened to my friend's sentences everything she said seem confused and mixed up. Her eyes so tired from crying. Sitting on my bed, so confused and innocent of what was happening. I watched her kneeling, holding her

Bible and pleading for forgiveness. I asked her why she would run away at 1 am in the morning with nothing but a winter nightdress on, walking 3 to 4 streets in the pitch dark. She never answered me. I remember the police woman asked both Megan and I questions. Had Megan ever told me anything? She hadn't really told me anything, but I did tell of one time, when playing in her house, seeing some boxes covering a hiding place. When I asked her why she had a hiding place hidden behind some large boxes.

"You must never tell, I beg you. It is where I hide from my father."

I remember thinking she was an only child; her parents were in their late 40's, a lot older than my parents. Her Mum was a sweet woman, a stay-at-home Mum of the 70's, cooking and keeping the house perfect. I envied Megan, as I was the eldest of 3. Megan's room was perfect; she had every doll you could buy and a wardrobe full of pretty dresses and shoes, yet she was a lovely, sharing girl. I could not remember a nasty word from her.

Looking back in time I remember watching as the police and child care workers drove her away. I never saw her again; as the years drifted away I came to learn that Megan had run away that night because she had been abused. She needed help. She was in a nightmare beyond my imagination. What I remember now was how brave she was at 10 years old to venture out in the 1970's, before her time, to stand up for herself even as painful as it was. I often wonder about Megan, and if she found peace. Knowing what she did on her own that dark night in 1978 was truly amazing and so brave. She is my Hero. I will always Treasure her undying friendship.

Another Nightmare I'm 5 again, I'm alone its dark, I'm lost in the bush. I can hear people fighting, gun shots ringing though the air like music. As I start to run, I feel the earth open up. I begin to fall at a slow speed. Then I hear the little Girl

"Wake up Katie. Wake up! It will be alright, just wake up!"

Chapter 3

Felicity

A woman standing naked in front of a mirror, studying her appearance, remembering that her breast once sat up high and when did her hips get so big? Looking at her face and feeling depressed, she pulls her face upwards, sighs, wishing she could turn back time... time and gravity. Now, noticing more grey hair, she reaches for the hair dye. After washing the dye out of her hair she lights candles and starts a bubble bath. As soft music echoes through the room, she grabs a glass of wine and relaxes in the bath.

"Good grief, I am not 50; I don't want to be an old woman just yet."

Emerging from the bath, she grabs a towel and looks in the mirror again, this time with determination, she sets about doing her hair and nails. She does her makeup in soft natural enhancing colours, keeping it light. Eyelashes come to life and bright red lipstick to match her nails. Walking from the bathroom, she enters a bedroom. A huge, very modern room with a fireplace, bar, flat screen television, computer and a massive wardrobe opening with 6 doors. Impressive set up indeed, clothes hanging in order of length, a chest of drawers and boxes and boxes of shoes labelled and in colour order. There were so many different wigs of many colours, length and styles. In one section of the wardrobe there were 100's of matching sets of lingerie in every imaginable colour and style. She looks around deciding what to wear, taking it back to the bathroom and changes.

Now standing in front of the mirror, is the same woman. This time what she sees is determination and confidence.

"What a great choice" she thought, checking her appearance, spinning around. She enters the bedroom, this time with confidence, she is the STAR.

The camera catches her every move, from her red 6 inch shoes, which make her legs look even longer and sexier in black fishnet stockings, to her cheeky little red shiny leather shorts and figure hugging red camisole, topped off with a black glittery suit jacket. With a waist length bright red wig, she is simply stunning for her age. Black sunglasses hiding her identity making her unrecognizable to those who know her, she is now FELICITY.

A far cry from the woman in the mirror, just a few hours ago. Felicity is a private dancer, a woman wanted by many men, performing private dances for hundreds. She is a new age performer, taking the cyber-sex world to a new level. Always classy and sexy, her costumes were always lacy, classy and sexy, delivering a mature classy performance. Wigs and large dark glasses concealed her identity. Her acts were top class, always wearing her trademark bright lipstick and nail polish. Her sexy outfits revealed only enough to make the imagination want more. Stopping and leaving you wanting more.

Never delivering a tacky show, she always stayed in control as she dances, moving her hips, striking a sexy pose. She has her viewers captivated by her every move, in her latest outfit. She poses dancing around; slowly showing her sexy, curvy middle aged body proudly. With her red wig as bright as her lips and shoes. All of a sudden an upbeat tune rung out in the room. She turns around and slowly removed her shorts, all to the beat of the music. Holding her jacket across her body, she turns and shows the shorts in her hands. Grinning, she gives a sexy wave goodbye before dropping them and pulling her jacket up as she dances, moving her hips so sexy. She reveals enough of her body to have even more viewers log on to her cam. Now she removes her jacket to reveal the red camisole and black stockings taking it to a new level.

She walks towards the camera and PC screen looking at all the messages flooding in. She smiles, blows a kiss, waves and dances away from the cam. She turns and pulls off the camisole revealing her lingerie. Her viewer numbers start to climb rapidly, as she stands there in her heels and lingerie. She is pure class. She removes her undergarments with her back turned then she turns slowly, revealing her naked body only for a few seconds, blows a kiss and waves goodbye and turns the cam off, leaving her captive audience wanting MORE.

Hundreds of men watching her cam captivated by her every move. She is the star, a far cry from the woman in the mirror only a few hours ago. She is Felicity a strong confident sexy middle aged woman who knows what she wants and how to demand all the attention.

Chapter 4

Melinda

Melinda woke early today, looking out her bedroom window as the sun came up. She saw her mother in the yard; a whole new garden patch had been dug. Gardening tools among the bags of seeds scattered on the ground, and there was Mable in her nightdress. She had obviously been up all night, just one of the many crazy things her mother did. Grabbing a blanket Melinda walked outside.

"Mum!" Melinda called as she saw her Mum

"Have you been up all night?" Mable looked up smiling.

"I did this" she replied. "See I can look after us. I wish your Dad was still alive" Melinda placed the blanket around her mother's shoulders and said softly

"Come on mum. Let's go in for a nice cuppa." Mable follows Melinda inside as if she is the child.

Melinda busies herself in the kitchen making the porridge and boiling the kettle, talking and acting as if she is the parent.

"Ok Mum lets have breakfast then maybe you should go back to bed after such a busy night in the garden. I have school soon. I will wake you when I get home at 3 pm. You have to work at Mrs Booth's dinner party and need to be there by 4."

Mable wanders off to get cleaned up, changes and crawls into bed. So, so tired but her mind just will not stop. Trying so hard to sleep, she would doze off but her mind would imagine something and her eyes would open widely. Fighting her mind as hard as she can, she finally finds peace in sleep.

Melinda quickly cleans up, finishing just as a there is a knock on the door.

"Phyllis you are early today" she says as she opened the door. Phyllis was the 3rd child of ten. The eldest girl, she had a lot of chores for a child so young. Every so often she would get away early, just to escape another thing she might have to do. She would come and pick up Melinda for School.

Deep down Melinda wished for normality like a Dad and siblings, she would not mind either brothers or sisters; she thought Phyllis was lucky to have such a big family. The girls took the long way to school chatting a hundred miles an hour, dancing, running and skipping along. They talked about everything and anything. They arrived at the school just as the bell sounded. Phyllis yelled out to her friend.

"Mel come over after school, mum said she will teach us how to make butterfly cakes."

Phyllis's Mum was a lovely woman she never judged Mable or Melinda. Her caring loving nature always shone through a busy lady with many children she always had time to help others and give what little she had. She loved to cook and sew; teaching her daughters was what she loved best. Melinda loved spending time with Phyllis and her mother, everything seemed normal at their very busy noisy house.

"Ok but I will have to go home first to check on Mum, I will see you about four." With that Melinda walked off to class.

"What a long day" thought Melinda?

She wished the bell would hurry up and ring 6 hours seemed like a lifetime to a child. Finally the bell rang - music to her ears; school was finally over for another day. Within 10 minutes the school was empty, all that could be heard was the echoing laughter of the children as they hurried off home to new adventures. Some days she dreaded going home she loved her mum but she just didn't know what to expect.

Every day was different with her mum, her moods and changing behaviour was so unpredictable. Mable had high days and low days, from laughter to tears in a heartbeat. What afternoons did bring was a new adventure, Melinda walked home alone today. Phyllis had got a lift with her dad who was in town. All of a sudden she sees a group of teenage boys, her heart sank. It was Tommy and his group of bully friends. She turned and went back the long way home along the creek. She didn't want to walk pass them. They had cornered her once before pushing and shoving her with name calling. The more she cried the nastier they and their chanting became.

"Crazy! Crazy! Your Mother's crazy. It's in her genes and it's in your blood. You're going to end up as mental as her" chanted the boys.

Luckily for Melinda, Mr Booth saw what was happening and broke up the disturbance, telling the boys off and giving her a ride home. So since then she had avoided kids and never drew attention to herself. Hurrying along she ran to the creek, heading home as fast as she could not looking behind her.

Mable had woken early and feeling a lot calmer, had gotten ready for work. She decided to prepare her daughters dinner, as she didn't finish work till around 9pm tonight. Leaving the front door unlocked, she left Melinda a note.

"Melinda – Dinner is ready. Eat early while it is still warm. Love you. I'll see you later tonight. xxxxxxxxxxxxxxxx Mum."

Mable hurried off to do a few errands on her walk through the town to the Booths Farm.

Phyllis sat at her window waiting for Melinda. The clock said almost 5pm. Phyllis wasn't too worried as she knew Melinda's mum often needed her. Phyllis's mother called her to go help with dinner. The young girl went off to help when all of a sudden she thought she heard her friend call out. She went outside for a second she thought she saw Melinda but there was no one there back inside she felt cold shivers down her spine it felt like something or someone was touching her. She could not explain the feelings she had or what had just happened.

Mable arrived home at 10pm. Some of the guests had given her a lift. Entering the house, she called out for her daughter. With no response she went to the girl's room. She found Melinda's bed empty and no sign of the little girl, her dinner was untouched.

She searched the whole house and then she started to panic and ran to a nearby neighbour's house, they had a phone. They called the police and her neighbour gave her a lift to Phyllis's Farm. All the sudden the whole street came alive as the news of a missing child circulated. The police went to Phyllis's home asking questions and tried to piece together the young girl's movements. Phyllis told them that her friend had not arrived. The police, along with a lot of the towns' people, begin searching the streets, parks and the school. People were calling out the Childs name waiting in vain for a response. Shortly after sunrise the search stops and the police arrived at Mable's home with news a mother never wants to hear.

The young officer stepped forward and with his head down to hide his tears saying

"I am so sorry Mable; we found her body near the creek. She was not alive, I am so, so sorry. Melinda's body has been taken to the hospital morgue we will need you to assist us in identifying her. Again I am so sorry for your loss."

Mable's face was totally drained of all colour and her mind went totally blank. She was as white as a ghost. Was her baby girl really gone, lying in a cold morgue all alone? Then Mable found an incredible strength, standing she stated very clearly
"I need to be with her NOW! My Baby needs me!"
"We will take you there now Mable" Constable Mathews answered, holding out his hand and leading her to the police car.

Neighbours stood around, some out of pity, others purely out of a morbid curiosity. The morgue was cold with all the furnishing in a very cold feeling stainless steel. It looked so bare and forbidding that it made Mable shiver as she entered a room where her little girl's body lay covered with a white sheet. For a second Mable thought she heard her daughter call out.

As the sheet was pulled back off the child's face, it was surprising how peaceful the little girl looked with no real sign of trauma, except for a small mark on the left of her forehead.

Her eyes were closed and she looked like she was sleeping but the cold hands on Mable's heart told her otherwise. Trying not to cry or show emotion Mable asked the young constable.

"Does anyone know how this happened?"

"We will conduct a few inquiries, but at this stage it looks like it could have been an accident" was his sad reply. He felt sad not being able to give this young mother the answer her heart ached for.

"Did she suffer? Where was she found? Who found her?" so many questions but none seemed important now.

Mable bent over to whisper to her beautiful daughter.

"Fly away my earth angel, become that special angel who helps people who are sad and lost." She remembers this being her daughters wish and she knew Melinda already had her angel wings for the rest of eternity.

"Fly back to me one day My Angel I will be waiting" Mable looked up through her tears, she was certain she saw her beautiful Melinda with long dark hair flawless skin and dark blue eyes, dancing though the cold corridor smiling, blowing a kiss to her.

Mable knew Melinda was special; she comforted herself thinking God needed another Angel, so he reached down to earth and took Melinda.

Chapter 5

Katie

Time moved on, but the nightmares had not. I was always 5 years old in my dreams, no matter how old I was in reality. Jolting up early one morning I was too scared to open my eyes, the dreams seemed so real and so violent. I hear screaming. It's my mother and a man is yelling at me. I can't see his face he is so big. He's calling me a dog, a filthy animal yelling abuse throwing things at me. I try to run but the chains are too tight around my neck I'm starting to choke. I plead with him to let me go, He won't listen he just pulls the chains tighter. I'm choking, no air, I can't breathe. Then I hear the little girl.

"Wake up Katie. Wake up! It will be alright, just wake up!"

I remember waking up so terrified, I was choking and gagging. So drained, my mind is on overload. I swear I can hear my heart beating. It is so loud; I am scared someone will hear it. Am I awake? Being 11 years old, it is hard. This is the only life I know and to me this is NORMAL. Why do I feel so sad? We move again and this time to N.S.W. where my life changed. The kids were different in the village. They belonged to Army families. Only they had their own groups and being a dorky eleven years old with dead straight hair, bat ears and a big nose. I was painfully shy and I was an easy target. I missed my SAYCA group and all my old friends, life became so hard here that I hated leaving the house. School was just awful.

The daily taunts, the nasty comments making me too scared to even ride my bike home as there would always be a group of want to be tough girls - a bunch of idiots, waiting for me. Yes, in the 70's bullies were around. Everyone knew it but it was totally ignored at school, and kids like me were too scared to tell our parents for fear of being harassed even more.

"Stand up for yourself." My Dad would say. Yeah, great words of wisdom. Telling a little 11 year old to stand up for herself against a group of 15 or more kids. Sorry, impossible. So I became paranoid of everything, I avoided everyone I could. There were a few scattered friends along the way they would always end up joining the enemy, soon becoming my tormenters too. I would go home, look in the mirror and cry. I hated how I looked. By age 13 I always looked washed out and tired. The vicious gossiping of the teens started and it became even worse. I really had no friends, no-one at all.

I become the local babysitter at 13, so my weekends were mainly busy. Perfect! Less time to be noticed. But now I had money, no friends, rotten headaches and was bored with my own company. Yep, puberty was knocking on the door. My mind would go so fast. I remember feeling myself boiling up with anger; I would be counting numbers - useless, stupid numbers. Grabbing at them, so frustrated with no escape. Except I did find an escape with three older girls. A cool bunch of girls in year 10, a bit on 'the naughty side'. We had lots of sleepover parties, they were awesome.

Linda's place was the best there was just her and her mother. Her Mum worked nights so "Yay!" no parents. If and when she was there she never bothered us. Finally I had friends, even cooler, they were nearly 16 and I was 13. Major ego boost! I remember on my 1st night Linda decided it might be fun to play 'spin the bottle' and then Theresa pulled out a flask. Linda poured it into a cup. "Yuk!" I remembered thinking, but I didn't want to be different so I joined the girls' game. I took my 1st drink of alcohol. After the 2nd drink it was easy and there was such a warm comfortable feeling, life seemed brighter and I felt like I could handle anything. Everything was funny and I felt so happy, surrounded by my friends.

Linda, Theresa and Nicole went to another High School in the next suburb; I met them at the local Friday nights youth Bible classes at the Baptist church. Even though they were older than me they were so friendly and nice and befriended me. Even on the breaks, I would sit with all my new friends. I would go home at night so happy I would be already looking forward to the next Friday night. I will always remember being so excited to go to those Friday night Bible classes; because I knew my trio of friends would be there. They didn't care what I looked like or who I was, they saw beyond all that, I know they valued me as a true friend. Linda's Sleepovers became a regular thing I loved going there and hanging out with the girls'.

The nightmares continued even though my days were much brighter and happier. Headaches, dizzy spells, frustration building over the simplest of things, so much anger, all the anger fighting so hard to be released.

Awake again, all hot and sweaty, my dreams seem so real. This time I am standing on a cliff edge. Looking over, I am 5 again. I remember this girl I went to school with her in Singapore. She is in my dream. She is nasty, screaming at me! My head is ready to burst from a headache she is forcing me closer to the edge of a very high cliff. Why does she hate me? Pushing me further to the edge - my foot slips. I began to fall off the cliff. I try to grab onto something, screaming, crying, I'm falling fast it seems like no end.

Then I hear the little girl

"Wake up Katie. Wake up! It will be alright, just wake up!"

Jolted awake yet again, so scared yet so calm, I knew they were only dreams and that in reality I was ok. But it was so hard when I was so young and in my mind so alone. My father was home a lot more here in N.S.W. and mum was always sad, when he was at home. Her eyes were always hidden under dark glasses; she would again be wearing long sleeves and pants in the middle of a hot summer.

Mum was so different when Dad was away. These were the only times she could have friends over and be herself. She would be so happy. It is the only time I can ever remember her smiling laughing and having fun.

Actually we were all much happier when Dad wasn't around. I had a father but never had a daddy. I envied girls who had a loving, caring dad. Kyle needed a dad who would teach him boy stuff and Lorna like I, needed a Daddy. Such a shame for us, this was typical of our parents' generation. You can't miss what you never had, that saying really isn't true. Every little girl deserved to be Daddy's little Princess.

Chapter 6

Felicity

Felicity enters the room, the cam is already on and hundreds of her fans are waiting. The PC screen is full of chats coming though. She never answers them, she just holds up a sign that simply says: "THANK YOU! I see all the messages."

She never speaks and you can only hear music. Standing there, she is wearing a long blonde wig with a fringe; a headband to match her purple and pink very short 1960s mini dress; hot pink sunglasses with hot pink boots and her signature bright lipstick and nails. Viewers begin logging on very quickly, the chat screen out of control. Phone numbers and offers from men pleading to meet her. She never answers them or gives out her phone number. One man offering her $20,000 to spend just one night with him. She laughs and starts dancing to The Kooks song "She moved in her own way" echoing loudly throughout her room. She did everything her own way and most defiantly moves her own way. Her cam tops in at 1100 viewers, men from every country want her and so many woman want to be her.

The numbers double as she starts to remove her clothes. Revealing her hot pink 1960's style lingerie; with bold black ribbons. She has her very own style, very classy. A new song starts The Kinks "You really got me". She moves to the music, making sure the cam angle is flattering - removing her lingerie as she dances. Just like she is dancing with someone. Teasing her audience with her every move she has the power, she controls them all. Standing facing the camera in just stockings and boots she blows a kiss, waves and then the cam turns off. Chats continue to light up her screen, even though she has already turned off the cam. She takes off the wig changes costume and freshens up her make up.

The cam is fired up again. Felicity now appears for your entertainment. This time, she is in a cheeky mood. Her costume is a clown - short curly red wig, yellow stockings with 6 inch yellow and red heels, yellow shorts and an oversized clown jacket. Complete with a giant tie and a round bright yellow hat with a big red flower sticking out of the top. She looks at her viewers, 525 watching at this time and clocking up fast. She laughs and says to herself

"These clowns will watch anything."

All of a sudden the music of "Send in the clowns" fills the air. Teasing her audience with her every move, she has the power. She controls them all. Nobody knows who she really is, nobody will ever know. Slowly removing her clothes, captivating her audience, she has them under her spell. Her screen is overflowing with men desperate to have her.

FELICITY I LOVE YOU! - From one of her many admirers.

She just laughs dances around some more. Felicity does not see faces, she does not want to. There would be no excitement or adrenaline rush in that. She is happy, hidden under her costume. She has the best of both worlds.

Viewers clocking up to 1800 hits, she is still not happy. She removes her jacket easily, yet so classy, revealing a bright yellow bra with big red Polka dots. Her audience is going insane. Hundreds of messages are flooding her screen. Viewers are up to 2100. Still not happy, she slowly removes off her shorts to reveal a matching yellow bootleg brief.

She looks at the messages and the guy who had previously offered $20,000 is now offering her $25,000! She laughs, she doesn't want their money. She does not do any of this for monetary rewards, just self-gratification and her ego. She removes her lingerie, turns to face the camera and then throws her sexy underwear towards it. She walks over blows a kiss, waves and shuts the cam off. The viewer's slowly drop off, but she knows they will be there when she signs back on.

Chapter 7

Melinda

Phyllis was sitting on the bank of the creek where her young friend Melinda's body had been found. She could still feel the warmth of her small friend's body. Crying she looks around, she could feel her friend holding her hand. She cried out "Melinda, don't leave me! We were supposed to grow old together, and rear our children together! What will I do without you?"

Suddenly Phyllis felt something touch her face; it was a soft, tender loving kind of touch. She did not feel threatened in any way. She jumped up looking around but no-one was there and yet she felt a presence. She walked over to the exact spot where her dear little friend had been found and she could see the blood on the rock.

Phyllis hears her friend call out and she turns and, as clear as day, sees her friend standing there smiling and waving to her. Phyllis dries her tears looks again, her friend is gone. She makes a solemn promise aloud and in her heart.

"Melinda I will always love you and I promise I will never forget you."

"Phyllis" yelled Ted, her older brother.

Ted hugged his younger sister and tried with all his heart to give her some form of comfort.

"Phyllis, it will be alright. At least you had the chance to be her friend and make a difference in her short life. I know she loved you" as he hugged her tight to his chest.

"You were the reason Melinda smiled and could face all the other kids at school, even face going home. She had a real true friend in you. Mum said to come get you. Melinda's funeral is at 1pm and her Mum wants to see you before."

Phyllis looked up her eyes so red and swollen from the non-stop crying since Melinda died; she felt like her heart would surely break and she too would die. All she could manage to say was

"Ok Teddy" she took his hand, following in a daze.

Phyllis and Ted arrived at Mable's house. She was alone, sitting in Melinda's room. She didn't hear Phyllis knock or come in. Mable smiled when she saw the young girl who, like her, had red swollen eyes she reached out to hold the little girl close to her.

"Hello Phyllis, how are you doing?" Phyllis started crying the tears just ran down her little face. Mable tried so hard to hold in her emotions and not cry. The strain of the last few days, losing Melinda was all too much to bear.

"Phyllis, we both need to be happy. We had known her, if even only for a short time. We were truly blessed by God. My daughter loved you unconditionally. I know she treasured your friendship. You protected her from the bullies; she will always be close to you. And I will always be grateful for the love you showed Melinda."

Mable took the young girl's hand and they walked into Melinda's room. Phyllis looked around the room wishing Melinda would walk in. The young mum reached inside the wardrobe, took out a small brown paper bag and handed it to Phyllis. Opening it, she saw the pair of little black boots her dear friend had loved and treasured so much. They had been lovingly cleaned and polished by the young mum on that dreadful heart-breaking night when they had been handed to her by the young police constable Mathews. Mable again became quiet and hung her head in silence.

"If only I had been a better Mother, she should not have been walking home on her own, and I should have protected her more. How will I go on, without my beautiful strong Melinda?" They cried, holding onto each other tightly, both of them feeling as if their hearts would break into a million and one pieces. Ted was standing quietly, waiting patiently for his little sister.

He wondered how both these people would recover from this lost, his heart ached for his young sister as he truly understood the love she had for her lost friend. Phyllis walked home with Ted holding, tightly to her precious gift and knowing she had a little part of her friend, and that as long as she lived; Melinda would always be in her heart and a huge part of her life. Ted tried to comfort his sister telling her time will heal, but Phyllis softly replied

"I don't want to forget her, ever."

Melinda's funeral was small, just a few close friends of Mable's, and a few teachers from the school. Mr and Mrs Booth were there. Not only had they given Mable time off, but they had paid for the funeral. Knowing Mable could not afford to bury Melinda. Phyllis sat in the front row, with her parents each side of her. She stared at the small white coffin covered in pretty white daisies, knowing her friend's lifeless body laid inside almost broke her heart. She wanted to open the coffin and yell 'Run Melinda, run'. The sermon was sad, but lovely.

She stood and watched in silence as her friend's tiny coffin was lowered into the deep hole. She slowly stepped forward and threw a pair of pretty white angel wings in with her friend. She whispered ever so softly,

"Fly back to me Melinda. I will always love you. Thank you for the best friend ever."

Back at Mabel's house for the wake, the young mother sat quietly not saying much. Even though she wasn't quite 32 she looked like an old woman and yet like a child. She sat with her hands folded on her lap, as if she could not move staring into space.

Phyllis's mum was there offering her love and support, as she too had suffered the loss of a young child. She knew that kind of pain and also the guilt of what I could have done or should have done. She had gone to town 6 years before while there, her young son 'Patrick'; 18 months old, had fallen into the fireplace. The older children had tried to pull him out, but it was too late. With a small tear running softly down her face, she returns to the present and to the sadness that now lay before this young mother and also before her daughter, Phyllis.

Mable left town shortly after the funeral and no-one ever heard from her again or mentioned her. Phyllis never forgot Mable and would never forget her 1st and only best friend Mel.

Life can be mean, hard to understand how things work. Why was someone so young taken so soon? Just one more minute to say goodbye, before she was pulled so quickly from earth...Leaving grieving family and friends behind, with a hole in their hearts that will never heal.

Chapter 8

Katie

Another night, another nightmare. My mother crying, I see her, she is screaming and a man is hurting her. She is covered in blood.

"Leave her alone," I plead. He hears me but refuses to listen. He just keeps on hurting and beating her, she stops fighting. I see her I'm right next to her but I can't reach her.

"MUM, Mum, I can't reach you. Run Mum get away. RUN."

I'm trying to run but all the sudden I can't move; my feet are stuck. I looked down I don't have feet. I'm standing in a pile of blood then the floor gives way, I'm falling, I can't stop myself, nothing to grab on to. I start to give up and stop fighting.

Then I hear the little girl,
"Wake up Katie. Wake up! It will be alright, just wake up!"

Jolting awake with fear, my head hurts the dream so vividly real. Why do I have these nightmares? I hated my life. I was nearly 14 and I was afraid to fall asleep in fear of what I might dream. My school life was crap so I started to jig school, go hang out with Linda. She had already finished school. What started as fun had turned into a way of life for me. When I was drinking I was free, it made me feel like I didn't have a worry in the world. Getting alcohol was easy in the 1980's. Linda had no problem at 17, nobody asked for ID back then. At any age you could buy cigarettes if the shopkeeper asked, you just said "They're for my Mum or Dad."

One day I told my friends about my nightmares. They didn't laugh, they understood. But my drinking binges were affecting my every move.

"I can stop whenever I want" I told my friends and worst of all, myself.

They simply replied. "You can, can you?"

But at that time in my life I did not want to stop as when I drank I didn't have nightmares, or at least I didn't remember them if I did.

"Go back to school" said Linda

"Katie, don't be a bloody idiot go back to school. You shouldn't listen to what those losers say. Try to make a go of it, study hard, and make a decent life for yourself - not just one about parties, fun and damn drinking."

I knew she was right. I had my whole life ahead of me, but the nightmares, fainting spells, crazy mood swings and the thought of that terrible school petrified me. I just wanted to hide.

"Ok I will think about it"

"No, not good enough, how long do you think it will be before the school rings your parents, Katie?"

Damn, I had forgotten my parents. Suddenly very terrified of my father, I agreed with Linda. I set off towards home to pick up Kyle and Lorna from their school knowing I would be so late, trying to think of excuses as I hurried along. I remember walking along the highway thinking how easy it would be to jump under a passing truck. No more pain, I would be free.

"Where have you been", said Lorna, wiping the tears off her face.

"Sorry sweetie, I missed the bus."

"Well that just sucks" piped up Kyle. He was always the one to come out with some smart ass remark. Laughing I reminded him we were not to use curse words.

"Yeah, I remember Katie, sometimes I just forget." With a wide cheeky grin, he rolled his big blue eyes.

"Little smarty pants" I thought as I walked towards the office to explain my lateness. Mrs Wilson swallowed my excuse, telling me it wasn't my fault the bus didn't wait. Little did she know she was being conned. Then we continued home. Come on kids lets go home taking their hands in mine.

"Katie" said Kyle, "Why do you smell funny? You smell just like that crap Mum cleans the bathroom with."

"Don't be so silly" was my short reply. Walking home, I realized I was staying around for these little guys, I had to protect them. Lorna was 6 and Kyle was 7. I had to protect them and look after them. Although I knew it was only nightmares, it still frightened me when I was wide awake. It was as if some strange haze fell over me.

"Who is home?" Lorna asked

"No-one." Dad went away this afternoon.

"Only mum?" She continued on.

"I hate it when HE is home" Lorna said.

"Me too" piped up Kyle.

"So we all agree then Dads an arsehole? I wish he would never come home."

"That is not nice Munchkin" I said, trying to hide the smile from my face.

"But" added my very wise little sister "Mummy's always so very sad when he is there and so happy and smiling when he is gone, I wished she would stay like that forever."

I tried so hard to explain that Mum was always so busy caring for all of us. But the sad cold truth is, that even as young as they were, they saw and heard more than anyone realized. And I then knew that they too carried a burden with them.

Finally - day becomes night and the Munchkins are fed, bathed and in bed. I sat quietly waiting for Mum, who had started work as a nurse in a local hospital. I'm sure it was a ploy to be away from our father more, she told us she needed the extra money, as Dad only gave her a little for food and bills. So now she can buy a few treats for us kids.

"Katie" Mum calls out as she opens the door.

"In the kitchen Mum, your dinner is ready".

"Mum!!!" I screamed "What happened to your face?" It was black, bruised and swollen, and her eyes were still red from crying.

"What happened?"

"Oh it's nothing really, I just fell in the bathroom at work" and I knew that would have been what she told them at work, that she had a fall at home.

"Bullshit!" I shouted back angrily knowing damn well what had happened.

"Please Katie, don't start. I fell, let's leave it at that."

I couldn't save her in my dreams and I couldn't save her now. She looked at me her expression changed. She looked worried, so concerned,

"Katie, the school rang today. Why haven't you been at school for the last 3 days?"

"Does Dad know?" I replied, terrified.

"No sweetheart, it is just between you and me, and that is how it will stay."

"Mum I hate school! I hate them all!"

"Sweetie, please be brave don't be afraid. Stand up for yourself. Don't let bullies dictate to you and affect your childhood or your future. You are a bright and beautiful girl Katie, and your future will be bright, I promise."

Mum wrote notes to cover me, "sick with a sore throat and headache" she wrote. And she went on to say

"Dad will never know, but I can't help you if it happens again please promise me you won't do this again, Katie." Her voice sounded hurt, angry and so very tired. I know she was scared of my Dad. I also knew she was disappointed in me.

Chapter - 9

Katie

Today I woke to another nightmare. My head was clear, but I felt so drained. Like someone is stealing my energy. As I hurry to get dressed for school, not really wanting to go, I hear a knock at the door.

"Katie your friends are here" Mum calls out.

Coming out I see Linda, Theresa and Nicole.

"We've come to drive you to school", Linda promptly announced.

Jumping up with excitement Nicole exclaims "I got my license yesterday Katie". We were screaming and dancing around like only teenage girls can.

Mum looks at me and I can see the fear in her eyes.

"Please make sure she goes to school today. Remember you promised Katie."

My heart skipped a beat thinking of going to school.

"No worries, Mrs G. That's why we are here" Linda says brightly.

Running out to the car, Nicole says "You get in the front Katie."

Driving towards the school Theresa must have sensed my mood.

"It will be alright Katie."

"How the fuck can you help me? I am alone in that fucking hell hole all day and you can't protect me once I am in the school grounds.

"We will take you and pick you up each day" and then they added that I had least would not have to ride the damn bus. I knew my dear friends really did mean to help; they were only trying to help me. I was so grateful by their friendship and their love towards me.

"You really would do that for me?" I asked

"For you Katie anything" Theresa added.

Now why couldn't they have just stayed at the school, instead of leaving me surrounded by complete idiots?

As we pulled up at the school, I saw a bunch of girls out by the front gates. I cringed as I got out. Smiling bravely at my three friends, I waved and walked towards the gates.

Walking pass the girls I could hear their evil phrase.

"God, do you see how big her ears are?"

"What ears? All I can see is the ugly troll" was another comment. Feeling my eyes well up with tears I started to run.

"Yeah, run you ugly bitch, you're scaring the dogs." Everyone was laughing at each others hateful taunts. Finally amongst the crowd, I hoped I would blend in and not be noticed.

It was a usual day for me. No-one spoke to me unless it was to be mean. Even going to the canteen was difficult, I could never get served as people constantly kept pushing in and I was always at the back of the line. And, as was often the case, I either had no lunch or the bell would go just as I was served. Again, no lunch. I had just turned around to get my bag when all I could see was a can being hurled towards me, hitting me right on the forehead just above the my eye. It was an opened can so there I stood, blood pouring from my head and with coke all over me.

I remember falling to my knees crying and blood everywhere. Dizziness, blurred vision, I was so scared I didn't know what to do. By now there was an even larger crowd of kids around me. Laughing and poking fun. No one even tried to help me or even went to get a teacher to help me.

"Just leave me alone!" I pleaded.

One girl called out "It's your fault you stupid cow!"

"How the hell is it my fault?" All I wanted was peace, I never hurt anyone. I could not understand their hatred towards me. All the faces became a blur to me and the pain from my head was unbelievable. Then all of a sudden I felt someone grab me, his name was Steven, an older boy about 16 years old, who I had seen around.

"Piss off you bloody idiots! Who the hell do you all think you are? Leave her alone." Then all the sudden he picked me up and carried me to the school office.

"Where is a damn teacher when you need one?" He yelled out as we entered though the office door.

"My goodness what happened?" Asked the school nurse - as she grabbed some gauze to stop the bleeding.

Steven looked at me I'm sure he could see the fear in my eyes. He said nothing just put me on the sickbay bed and smiled.

"I will talk to you later Miss Katie" Oh my goodness he knew my name and how handsome he was.

Lying in sick bay, I had 3 butterfly clips in my head holding my wound together and ice packs to stop the swelling. I stuck to my story that I had tripped and fallen. Let's face it, they treated me like shit now, what would they do if I dobbed on them? Things would be more unbearable.

I heard the school bell ring; I waited until I thought everyone had left before I attempted to leave. I grabbed my bag and headed out to meet Linda and the girls. As I got to the front door of the office I saw Steven standing there, I didn't want to see or talk to him so I ran out the back way and hurried out to meet the girls.

"Holy fucking hell Katie! What the fuck happened to you?" Linda screamed. I told them my story.

"Fucking arseholes" Theresa commented.

"Who were they?"

"Katie who was it?" They all asked at once. I told them I honestly did not see any one person.

"Katie you have to tell the teachers" said Nicole.

But I explained that would only make it worse if I dobbed on people.

"Please, just take me home."

On the way home I sat quietly day dreaming of Steven my Knight who saved me. I couldn't stop thinking about how handsome and strong he was. Was he waiting for me? - I convinced myself he wasn't there waiting for me, he didn't like me he just felt sorry for me. And he too would eventually join the enemy against me.

Chapter - 10

Felicity

Waking up from her sleep is the woman in the mirror. She is back in the real world. Looking at herself in the mirror she sees her age, her face free of makeup, her natural hair. Sitting back she smiles at the fuss she causes when she goes on cam.

"What a hoot!" She says out loud.

"I love it!" Just then a song comes on the radio – 'I am Woman.'

♫*Oh yes, I am wise*

But its wisdom born of pain

Yes, I've paid the price

But look how much I gained

If I have to

I can do anything

I am strong (strong)

I am invincible (invincible)

I am woman♫

She sings along to the chorus knowing all the words.

"Yes I am!" She is in total control of her own destiny and she knows it. She can be whomever she wants to be though the cyber world. Her life is blessed, to her she has it all and no one knows her secret. Sitting down with her morning coffee, she reads all the emails she has received. Sometimes she laughs out loud, but some verge on the ridiculous or insane. She answers them all with a smiley face and some kisses.

'☺ Felicity xox'

The woman in the mirror goes about her daily routine happily knowing she is strong, fearless, and untouchable; almost invincible. Checking her giant wardrobe, she moves things around trying to come up with new ideas for costumes, something new she hasn't done yet. She has hundreds of matching lingerie already but she wants more. There are 180 different pairs of shoes, every colour and style you could imagine.

Laughing out loud, she suddenly thinks a 'witch' - now that would be cute and sexy. She jumps online to look for ideas and material. Felicity has designed and made most of her lingerie and costumes, to keep in tune with her aging figure and to camouflage parts of her body she would rather not have on show. She wants to be her age, look her age, but in a mature classy way. To show the cyber world she still had lots of sex appeal and she is not afraid to let it show, at least not in front of the camera with her real identity hidden. Felicity is smart; she knows a fake tan would enhance her body features - stay up stocking hide her veins making her legs look sexy and shapely. Pulling her hair up tightly in a wig cap smooths her face, giving her face a younger look. Designing her lingerie to compliment her figure in just the right way; bootleg and briefs are way sexier on a mature woman.

She never wears anything personal like jewellery of any kind. Just in case someone could recognize her. She just didn't know who was part of her fan club could even be people she knows or has met. She never shows her face, always keeping the camera at an angle as not to show too much of the real her. She has created an illusion of mystery, seduction, a figment in all her audience's imaginations. It excited her and amazed her that so many people watched her; they were just a bunch of chat names to her. She was truly afraid of crowds, hated any form of live performances. She just wanted her internet fans, her own stage and never having to speak to or see anyone. She wasn't a MILF and hated being called a cougar. She was the one chased. She realized she had a hidden sex kitten in her, lost early in her life and found again in these later years.

She wanted to be loved and treated like a movie star. She wanted all that but still to be unknown. And now with this strange world of the internet she could have it all. She was wanted by so many and none of them were aware of her private world. She whispered to herself

"YOU ARE A PRIVATE DANCER – You are Felicity."

Chapter 11
Katie

My peaceful sleep is over, taken over by
nightmares. I am 5 again. I'm crying and I'm lost. I
am yelling but no-one hears me. Oh no I'm in a Box
I try to get out I can't, the lid is locked shut. I try
screaming no sound comes out. I'm trapped! There
is no air! I can't breathe! I hear laughing, evil
laughing. Please somebody hear me! Now the box is
filling up with rats they are biting me viciously. I'm
so scared, so helpless. I try to knock the rats away
but it is hopeless there is way too many. I begin to
give up fighting. Then I hear the little girl,

"Wake up Katie. Wake up! It will be alright, just
wake up!"

I slowly open my eyes, hoping I am awake.

"Get up Sleepy head!" I can hear giggling.

I look up to see Kyle. I am so relieved to see him,
I smile throwing my pillow at him

"Rack of hairy legs - hey Munchkin. I love you".

"I love you more sleepyhead" he replies with that obnoxious grin of his. Goodness I think what a handsome man he is going to be.

I hear laughter so I head to the kitchen, where Mum is standing there smiling. She looks so pretty, with a wide smile with a twinkle in her eyes. My mum had eyes that almost sang to you, when she was happy and smiling.

"School holidays!" Thank God was my only thought. I reminded Mum that I was sleeping at Linda's tonight.

"I remember, Katie, but I do worry that they are a little too old for you".

"But they are my only friends and they always look after me".

"Okay but promise me you will behave and don't do anything stupid" Mum added with concern.

It was so lovely to have our Mum happy it was so obvious, that our father was not home. In a way it was sad that she was only happy when he wasn't home. But how can a young girl wish her father not be around anymore? I just knew life would be happier for us without him.

I helped with all the housework while the little ones just watched and made another mess. God some days I loved theses little guys to pieces and other days I wished they weren't born yet.

'BEEP BEEP' The sound of Linda and the other girls pulling up in the driveway. Grabbing my bag and kissing everyone goodbye. I ran out to Nicole's car smiling with excitement. As I got into the backseat Theresa handed me a bottle of rum, which I had no problem opening and drinking it as fast as I could, it felt so good.

"I thought you could quit?" said Linda.

"I can," I said, "I just don't want to."

"Hey guess what?"

"What?" was the reply

"I am getting my ears fixed!"

"How... when?" They all chorused together.

"There is a new operation that can be done when the person is physiologically affected. Mum got Dad to ask the Army if we were covered with the health cover. It will cost nothing - And I have to see a Physiatrist Doctor then a Plastic Surgeon. YAY me I get to have normal ears."

"When... where?" The girls were so excited for me.

I explained that the surgeon said that they make an incision behind each ear and remove fatty tissue that is causing the ears to stick out and stitch them to my head.

"No more Katie with bat ears!"

I then went on to tell them that the operation was the following Tuesday, and I was going to the Private Hospital. They were all yelling.

"Oh that's so cool Katie... I'm so happy for you, but you know we love you the way you are" Nicole shouted above all the talking.

"No joke, hey I know. I love you girls more" I replied. "But you can bet those bitches at school will come up with something else to pick on me for."

All my frustration and built up anger faded when I was with these girls. They were truly my friends and my confidants - of course the booze helped. The pain that raged within me was lessened, and even when it came back, as I knew it would, I was at least free for now.

"Shit, Katie, slow down girl!" Linda warned "You are drinking far too much, and that's not good for you girl."
"Fucking bullshit, not enough" I slurred.
"For Christ sake, leave her alone Linda" Nicole said.

"Well if she chucks up, it is your car and it'll be your problem." Was Linda's reply.

I could not stop laughing.

"It's ok Linda, if that happens I will just flap my ears and fly away" slurring my words so much, I wasn't even sure what I just said.

"Oh you are fucking hilarious Katie!"

"Well the others thought I was funny." With that, Linda snatched the bottle off me.

"There will be no more until we are at my place. I do not need you making a scene out the front of my place."

"Okay Linda, you party pooper" was my reply, as I blew a raspberry then I couldn't help but burp very loudly and unladylike.

"Oops, geez that was loud, I think I heard an echo with theses giant ears."

By this time, I was giggling uncontrollably.

"Bloody hell, Katie" roared Nicole with laughter.

Pulling up in Linda's driveway I was so happy to be here with my friends.

"Yay, Linda's house" I yelled very loudly.

"Just shut up Katie, until we get inside" was the angry reply.

As usual no-one was home at Linda's. Her Mum had a new boyfriend and had gone to his place for the night. God, I was so lucky Mum had never asked to meet the girl's parents. But then I felt guilty that she trusted me, and here I was doing the worst thing I could do. My love for these girls outweighed any of the guilt. They were like sisters, in some ways even better than sisters. Sisters are often tittle-tats, but not these three. They made my life worth living. They gave me a reason to live; they never judged me or made fun of me. My time with them was so awesome, even without the alcohol.

My mind was like I was in a thick fog, endless thoughts, constantly rolling, remembering the mean kids at school, vicious gossip, those daily taunts. My nightmares torturing my sleep and every waking thought. It is so hard to fully explain where my head was. My feelings boiling up, just like the old fashioned gas heater we had in our bathroom at home, ready to blow up. Would I ever find peace within my own mind? Would I ever feel NORMAL?

I came to believe this was normal for me and there was nothing I could do except just live with what I had to deal with. I focused on my upcoming operation. And I thought it might be nice to change my hair maybe buy some new clothes as I was getting bigger and growing out of most of my stuff. I had a little money saved up. This thought at least cheered me up a little...

Chapter 12

Melinda

It was 11 years since the death of Phyllis' dear friend, Melinda. As she sits beside her grave this morning, she is missing her friend so much more than ever, even though the years have gone by so quickly her love for Melinda never did. All of a sudden a loud voice rings out.

"Hey Philly!" yells Ted, as he spots her sitting next to Melinda's grave.

He knew she would be here today of all days. As she grew up she spent less time at the grave but when she did, she would sit for hours chatting about the latest fashion; music; and the latest movie star. She told Melinda of the new Elvis movies, new songs and even showed her new dance steps. She told Melinda everything just like she had when she was alive. Deep within her heart, she knew her little friend heard her every word.

"Hi." Ted said again when she turned and noticed him standing there. "Mum said to come get you! Good God girl! You are getting married today! Did you forget?"

"Oh yeah like I had forgotten. I just wanted to tell Melinda all about the wedding and my future husband."

Phyllis was marrying a young soldier, Donald after meeting him only 6 weeks ago. She had met him at a local dance in Brisbane. He was going overseas soon and seemed in a hurry to make her his wife before he left. Phyllis was a Registered Nurse in one of the local hospitals, where she had completed her training 3 years ago. She wasn't sure if she truly loved him, he seemed so nice and kind but for some reason she didn't feel it was right. Yet it had felt like the right time to settle down. She was 23 and that was considered old in 1965. Donald did say he loved her with all his heart and Phyllis thought that was enough.

Phyllis told Melinda how she wished she was still alive as she would have been her Matron of Honour and that her Bridesmaids dresses were mauve, Melinda's favourite colour. The flowers were daisies - Melinda loved daisies. Phyllis just knew Melinda would be smiling at that.

"Come on Phyllis, time to go", said Ted, as he held out his hand to his little sister, about to take one of the biggest steps of her life.

Back at Phyllis Parents' house, it was a buzz with activity. People were everywhere.

"Where have you been Girl?" Her Mum asked, trying to stay as calm as the mother of the bride can be.

"Sorry Mum I had to see Melinda."

"Well move it now" said her mum, pushing her towards the shower.

Everything was ready for the bride to be. Laid out on the bed where her shoes, her stockings, her pretty Posey of fresh daisies tied with a mauve ribbon - which were to be placed on her Melinda's grave after the ceremony as Phyllis was getting married at the church near the cemetery. Phyllis was to wear her Aunt Anne's dress which was plain with long lace sleeves and a rather high neckline. It had a full skirt of delicate handmade lace. The only annoying part was the huge hoop that was worn underneath to hold out the gown. Ever since her Auntie Anne's wedding, she had wanted to wear this gown on her own day; her aunt had promised her she could. At the time she was only 13 but Phyllis had been so excited and now here she was! Standing in the gown she had dreamt about for many years!

Today was so full of mixed emotions; she wasn't sure why she felt so sad when she should have been happy and excited. An hour later she stood in front of the mirror, staring at herself. She could not believe this beautiful bride she seen in the mirror was her. Ted came into the room and for once stood - if only for a second - with his big mouth wide open.

"Oh Boy, Phyllis you look so beautiful! Who would have thought you would grow up into such a beautiful woman." He laughed then turned serious with a worried look.

"He had better be good to you or I will hunt him down, I promise you!"

"It will be ok Ted. Donald is a good man. I am sure we will be happy. I am just nervous, that is all" she smiled at her big brother. Ted was more than a big brother he was her best friend and protector she loved him to pieces.

It was a beautiful sunny August day in 1965. It was to be a small church service, with the reception at the local hall. There had been little time to organize a large event as the courtship had been very fast. He had proposed 3 weeks after they met.

"Something old, something new, something borrowed and something blue." Her Mum said the something borrowed was the dress; something blue was the pretty lace hanky Auntie Anne made; new was her white bridal shoes. Now, Phyllis thought, what could be the something old?

Running to her wardrobe she took out her friend's little black boots. Her Mum laughed.

"Love, they are hardly going to fit you now and they certainly do not go with the dress!"

Removing the laces, she lovingly tied them around the stems of her bridal flowers and she just knew Melinda was smiling down at her. She was still a big part of Phyllis's wedding dream as they had planned their wedding day's years ago as little girls.

Just then her Dad walks into the room. He smiles.

"Phyllis, you look so beautiful! Just like your Mum did on our wedding day." Crying slightly he adds

"Where has my little girl gone?"

He holds out his arm to his young daughter.

"Your chariot awaits, my Princess". Walking out into the sunshine to a 1960 JAG her dad hired for the day - it had a beautiful mauve ribbon and a bridal doll her Mum made.

Her 2 younger sisters were the bride's maids. Just as Phyllis was about to get into the car, she looked up and was certain she seen Melinda. Standing there near the second JAG blowing a kiss and waving like crazy...

Smiling to herself she thought today was going to be perfect - she was now certain Melinda was there with her...

Chapter 13

Felicity

Lights, camera, action! Music began playing loudly in the background. Viewers were logging on quickly, even before the lights came on. The lights flash quickly and you can see glimpses of purple and black.

All of the sudden, the music changes to the tune "Monster Mash" and a spotlight reveals Felicity, the sexy witch.

A huge witch's hat covers her head, with black and purple feathers around the brim. Her wig is a very long shiny straight, jet black colour. She wears her trademark matching bright nails and lipstick. Her dark sunglasses - purple with cobwebs around the rim and a cute, short, frilly, black skirt with ruffles of black lace underneath. A cute purple camisole with a see-through black coat covered in purple cobwebs, with matching purple and black feathers around the neckline and cuffs.

Black fishnet stockings and ankle high heel boots tied with purple ribbons. Completes Felicity's sexy witch; done her own way...

Felicity leans forward to see the number of viewers who have already tuned in; her viewers have reached over 900 already. She slowly walks away from the cam to reveal her sexy outfit. Dancing slowly to the 'Monster Mash' – smiling seductively as she dances.

She dances seductively to the music as only she can. Unclipping her coat, she turns around. You can see through the material, which of course is quite intentional. She again turns to face the cam. Opening up the coat, she reveals what's underneath. The viewer numbers shoots up suddenly to 2,500 - her highest yet. Messages are flooding onto her screen:

'OMG'

'NO WAY ARE YOU OVER 25'

'MARRY ME'

'I THINK I LOVE YOU'

'NOW THAT'S WHAT A REAL WOMAN SHOULD LOOK LIKE'

Removing her coat and skirt so everyone can see, her lingerie was a corset in black with purple cobwebs and ribbons. Sexy black boot leg briefs which tied up at the side with purple ribbons showed off her body to perfection. She knew how to work that cam and those viewers. Felicity was daring, cheeky, sexy all rolled into one. Loving the attention, knowing she was the Star and proud of whom she was.

She continued her dancing, removing her lingerie in a classy mature - oh so very sexy way. Now she was only in stockings, boots and briefs. She slowly removes her underwear to reveal a fake purple tattoo spider on the top of her pants line. Her chat screen now totally out of control:

'OMG SEXY'

'I WANT YOU'

'$20000 FOR A NIGHT WITH YOU'

'I HAVE DIED AND GONE TO HEAVEN'

The messages flooded her screen. She knows she is the Star. She laughs and walks away turning back to face the cam, she blows a kiss, waves goodbye as her viewer's reach 3,800. She shuts the cam down and wanders off to the shower.

An hour later, the woman in the mirror returns in her P.J.'s and slippers with no makeup on, looking natural. She laughs out loud as she wonders what all her internet fans would say if they saw her now. If she turned on the camera now, not one soul would take the least bit of notice in her.

She goes downstairs to the kitchen, makes a hot coffee then heads back to her laptop, this time she logs onto her Facebook. Another Inbox message from this guy saying simply;

"Hi stranger, how have you been?"

Who the hell is this guy? She honestly had no idea, but he has been sending messages every now and then over the last 3 years. Checking out his profile she sees they once lived on the same street in the same town, attending the same high school. He was 2 years older than her according to his profile age. Thinking she will just ignore his messages, anyway he hasn't tried to add me as a friend. She used her married name not her maiden name as she didn't want to be in contact with people from school. She was pretty sure He had her confused with someone else.

The woman in the mirror was so different from Felicity. This woman was like millions of others. Just like you maybe a wife, a mother, a daughter, a grandmother just trying to live a normal life and grow old gracefully never drawing attention to herself just going through life quietly. No one knew of her double life. She never told a soul. Crawling into bed; dreaming of her double life and internet stardom. She smiled thinking about her next show and thinking about her messages from all the fans. She did love the fans after all - if it wasn't for them she wouldn't be Felicity. Dreaming of her next costume...

Chapter 14

Katie

The next year will remain a blur to me. Drinking heavily at night and going to school in a permanent haze. I am not sure if the taunts became less or I just became immune and simply didn't care anymore.

Another nightmare haunts my sleep. I can see myself, I'm 5 again, and I'm cowering in the corner of a room. I can actually see myself. I'm floating above my little 5 year old body. My body is covered in bruises, bleeding, crying uncontrollably - I feel her pain but I'm not in pain. I just look at myself so little so fragile. Someone is approaching me. I'm scared, I want to run away. I scream out loudly.

"I'm sorry! Please don't hurt me." Then when I think I can't take any more torture. I hear the little girl...
"Wake up Katie. Wake up! It will be alright, just wake up!"

Waking up from this dream I am so exhausted. It's as if the stronger the nightmares become, the more they drain me and leave me lethargic. As exhausted as I felt, I wasn't scared so much anymore; I was just plain worn out. Why did I have these horrific nightmares? What did they mean? I can remember every nightmare in detail, I feel like I was lost in a haze.

"Get up sleepy head" Kyle yells out, poking his head around my bedroom door.

"Rack off hairy legs!" I yelled at him, "I love you"

"Love you more!" was his cheeky reply as he ran for cover.

Climbing out of my bed, I had an overwhelming feeling of anger washing over me. I was thinking about how mean the kids at school had been. How I wished I could just drift through this miserable life invisible. My looks were starting to improve. I had my ears pinned back and that had made me feel better, more confident. I had my hair cut to shoulder length and shaped around my face. My body it was going through its own changes. My skinny frame was beginning to fill out and become a womanly shape, my nose seemed to be smaller and more in portion with the rest of my face. Dark circles under my eyes - a combination of nightmares and alcohol was easily covered by makeup. I was now learning to do my eyebrows which were now 2, and how to do my makeup to highlight my best features. Mum said I look so pretty and I realised I was becoming a WOMAN!

I still wasn't sure of myself and not at all that confident with the new Katie. But all of a sudden people were starting to talk to me and in a nice way. A few girls even started to be friendly. But with a history of the bullying still vivid in my mind, I didn't trust anyone and kept my distance - preferring to spend my lunch time in the library. I usually read love stories and daydreamed of a Prince Charming carrying me off on his white horse.

One title I was reading was Independent Woman; chasing a dream, and her sexual encounters. Dreaming of the first time with my 'Prince' and not having a clue of what sex really was. Yes, of course I knew, but no one can know really just from reading books and from what other people tell you. Sitting in the library, my solitude and self-isolation appealed to me. Daydreams were my escape through the haze of nightmares and alcohol.

I would often wake from a nightmare, lock my door and climb out of my bedroom window and go for a walk at 1am or even later. I was never scared as I figured my nightmares were much worse than anything outside. I felt at ease almost as if I wasn't alone, as I obviously was. I could walk in utter silence as the world around me was sleeping. The Army village was still, except for a few dogs. I would be careful not to trigger them off or let them see me because I didn't want to draw attention to myself. If a car did happen to drive by - which was rare in the village after midnight, I would hide behind a bush, parked car or a fence. I become very good at camouflage. I would walk for hours in the early morning. Clearing my head and walking quietly back home again.

Under the house directly under my bedroom window; I had a small box, that was hidden behind a few bricks, which no one could see from outside. Inside was my stash of alcohol and my latest habit of destruction, smoking. I would sit under my window in the pitch dark, having a drink and a cigarette. I was - in my eyes - old enough to do what I wanted, even if I was only 15. Seriously, how could I be scared or care anymore; my nightmares were already a living hell! How can the dark or anyone scare me anymore?

Although one night I had an eerie feeling like someone was warning me, I climbed back into my bedroom window. Just as I locked it I saw a man walk into the backyard only seconds after. He looked around the backyard checking in the shed, after a short while he walked off again. He didn't scare me, just made me glad that I had climbed back in when I did. Maybe he had seen me and was following me. I did not recognize him in the dark; this was very common in the Army village. When husbands were away on manoeuvres, so many wives were frightened and would often not sleep or have other wives and their kids stay with them. Mum told me a story of how when I was little and in the bath, I had seen a man's hand at the window. My screaming had made him run off.

I remember when I was 10 - when we lived in Queensland. The houses were up high with a laundry and garage underneath, my Mum was downstairs in the laundry at about 7pm. Dad thought he heard something and went downstairs to check if Mum was okay. As he reached the bottom of the stairs, Mum was starting to come up. Suddenly he saw a man turn and run off. If My Dad had not gone downstairs when he did, god knows what would have happened to Mum! Just the thought of it still makes me feel sick to my stomach.

The man ran off, but he had to have known she was there, as the laundry lights were on. He must have been watching her and maybe thought our father was away.

My Dad called the police; both my parents had to make statements. I could, and so did they, see the footprints leading from the old style garage into the laundry. Where my mother had been standing oblivious to what was or could have happened. The police said it was obvious Dad had interrupted him and saved Mum from god knows what. From that day forward Dad checked every door and window several times over and made sure the garage and laundry doors were always locked. No need to say, but Mum never went downstairs at night again. It haunted our mother for years and years. Just the thought of what could have been. Her biggest worry was that I could have been with her, as I often was playing alongside the laundry in the dark...

My nightmares to me were much more terrifying! Were these stories causing my nightmares? My body was exhausted, but full of built up anger. I would eventually fall back to sleep after the walk. The alcohol and the cigarettes must have helped as my dreams seemed less scary and not as important.

Chapter 15

Felicity

Writing on her Facebook status, Felicity reminds them all she is only here to entertain herself. Then the woman in the mirror laughs out loud. If they only knew, she thought. They wouldn't believe her. Her life is so real and different, a far cry from this - her double life as Felicity. She really loved things the way they were. She got to be a star and have her kind of fame plus her loyal fans. She was very attractive for her age yet no one would mistake the woman in the mirror for a soft porn star. She wore clothes modern and classy, showing a mature sexy look but always age appropriate. Her body looking good but always covered. She knew she was sexy, but at the same time she never drew attention to herself in public. Never mixing or confusing her two personalities together. The woman in the mirror has a few close friends and tends to isolate herself, never seeking out people. She certainly is not an overly social person. She often laughs to herself proud that she is a loner. It is so much nicer to have a few close friends than a heap you either don't like or trust. The woman in the mirror needs to have full trust of those close to her. To her, most people and their opinions don't really matter anymore.

'Lights, camera, action!' The viewers are clocking up already. Felicity is here for your entertainment.

She enters the room dressed all in white. Tonight she is an angel. It is a 1900's style dress covering her from her neck to her toes, with big flowing sleeves - the white dress is slightly see through. Her Wig is light blonde with long ringlet curls and a gold Halo sits on top of her head. When she dances around you can see her cute little gold angel wings and her signature bright nails and lipstick. It doesn't take long for her fans to see she is online - viewers clocking up quickly to 800... People wait to see her knowing what time she comes online.

Because she can't see any faces it's like she is alone in her own world. Felicity is confident and knows what she wants. Her style is so complex, always acting her age, yet so appealing. With her fans ranging from their 20's all the way into their 70's. She certainly demands attention. So many of them fall under her spell, and so many messages flood her screen:

'YOU'RE AMAZING!'

'SIMPLY DEVINE'

'TALK TO ME'

So many men messaging their phone numbers. She never answers them and she never speaks. She just blows a kiss and waves occasionally. She is so comfortable in her cyber world she has created for herself. Walking around completely unknown... yet so famous. She is finding that other women are trying to imitate her; stealing her looks and style. But there is only room for the original Felicity.

She is a sweet angel, as she dances to the song:

♫*Hey Angel*

How do you feel right now?

How does it feel to be alone?

How do you feel right now?

Tell me

Hey angel - what's your situation

Hey angel - oh, oh, OH

Where would you be right now?

Waiting to taste your next tomorrow

Where would you be right now?

Tell me

Was the pain too strong to take it anymore?

So you turned off all the lights and shut the door

Hey angel - what's your destination

Hey angel

Hey angel - got a complication

You're my angel - angel - oh, oh, oh, oh, oh♪

That song was so sweet yet it summed her up perfectly. Then the music changes the song is now 'Oh Hark'. She absolutely loves this song!

She lets the music lead her as OH HARK is about an Angel who becomes mislead and runs off to be a Dark Angel. Then half way through the song, the cam zooms to her feet. As she lifts the dress, she reveals black high heels, black stockings with designer holes, a black leather and lace - tattered yet stylish tutu. To her leather black bra and hands now wearing long black leather gloves. The pretty angel wings are gone now replaced with black tattered wings. Her wig is now a raven black with messy curls. The white angel is now a dark angel, but she is so very sexy. Her red lips are now painted black. She dances raunchier now, blows a kiss and waves.

Then the messages start coming in:

'JUST WHEN I THOUGHT YOU COULDN'T GET ANY SEXER YOU GO AND PROVE ME WRONG'

'PLEASE LETS MEET'

'NO WAY YOU'RE NEARLY 50, MORE LIKE 25'

'I DO BELIEVE I HAVE DIED AND GONE TO HEAVEN'

She laughed at that last comment... There were so many messages flooding her screen. Most were flattering, some very disturbing. But she was safe; no one knew her true identity no one could find her.

Her style was unique. Many tried but failed to impersonate her looks and her style. She was indeed the Marilyn Monroe and they were Jayne Mansfield's. She danced around removing her tutu, her lingerie and her wings. Standing facing the cam; in just her stockings, shoes and gloves. She blows a kiss, wave's goodbye and shuts the cam off. Felicity runs off to change back into the Woman in Mirror...

Chapter 16

Katie

I started Year 10 today. Hey, how good is that? For the 1st time in my entire school life here I was excited about going to school. Now the kids had eased up and some had left. At last, I had a chance to start learning.

Walking from my room to the kitchen, I heard Mum. She sounded happy. She is singing and laughing with Lorna and Kyle, a sure indication that Dad was away. We kids loved it when he was away. Mum was happy - she was wearing makeup and pretty clothes. She wasn't hiding behind dark glasses and wearing long sleeves or jumpers. She really was so pretty standing there laughing with Lorna and Kyle. I wished she could always be happy. Sometimes I wished Dad wouldn't come home. Not that I wished him any harm, more like I wished he would simply disappear.

Kyle was now 10; cute as a button and getting cuter by the minute. Such a good looking boy with almost white blonde curly hair, deep blue eyes with long lashes and such a natural olive skin. He was cheeky, outspoken, annoying, gorgeous and loving - all rolled into one unique package.

Lorna was the exact opposite. She was always quiet and kept to herself, not wanting or needing to be with other kids her age. Her hair was jet black so long and thick. Mum always had it tied up in 2 plaits. Her huge eyes were brown, almost black. Her complexion was fair. She would spend hours in her room chatting to herself. I once asked her who she was talking to.

"Just my friends; they don't live here." I had to laugh at her wonderful imagination.

"Good morning Katie! You look so pretty today, my darling."

"Awe thanks, Mum. But mothers have to say that!"

"Well not this mother, I mean it, young lady." Came her instant reply.

"Mum on a different subject, let's move."

"Katie, I am sure the Army will move us soon enough. We have been here a fair while now."

"No Mum. I meant let's move away from Dad; I am old enough to know you aren't happy when he is around and you actually know what I'm talking about."

She looked at me, now with that sad frightened face she had when he was home.

"How can we Katie? He would find us and the Army would make sure he did. No darling, as hard as it is for you to understand, I think it is better if we stay."

"But Mum I love you and I know you aren't really happy."

"Enough, Katie! Just leave it alone. I am on afternoon shift today and need you to get the kids from school. Just do that for me please and I will get dinner done." Changing the subject as she suddenly turned serious - I felt so bad that I had made her sad again.

"Sure Mum. I know you told me last night but how long is Dad gone for this time?"

"6 weeks" she said, smiling. "Now remember, Kyle has cricket practice at 4pm. Mrs Hanlon will pick him up and drop him off around 5.30."

6 weeks! Awesome! That was like months to a 16 year old. I was hanging out less with my three older friends by this stage. We had simply grown apart, but in a nice way. We still spoke on the phone often. Linda, now 19, was working full time in one of the local banks. Nicole somehow had got into Uni - a miracle I reckon. And she had plans to be a teacher. This made me laugh whenever someone mentioned it. Theresa had met a young man and had got herself

engaged with little time left for friends. Now they were older and able to drive they had more independence and our time together had just become more limited. My life stayed the same, midnight walks, drinking and smoking. I still had no close friends at school, so I kept my secrets well hidden. The only person I could trust was *me*. Now my looks were changing and I had grown considerably in the right places. I could hear people whisper:

"Who's the new chick?"

"Wow she's spunk!"

When they heard it was me, Katie Green, the answer was always the same -

"No fucking way that is her!!"

I remember thinking what a bunch of shallow creeps. But life was easier, at least at school.

One night Theresa rang. Her fiancé Mark was helping out at his church where a disco for the local kids 13 to 18 was being held. At first I said no, I hated those events, but Theresa could be very persistent, so I finally decided to go. It would mainly be kids from other schools, so I may not know many of them anyway. The disco was the usual setup for the early 80's. I even remember exactly what I wore. I felt so positive, and one hour later I was ready.

A bone coloured satin shirt with a brown skirt and brown high heel boots. Looking in the mirror, I wondered where that ugly girl had gone. Standing before me was a stranger; and a pretty one at that. Theresa picked me up at 6.30pm as Mark was already there, getting everything set up for a well-organized, safe and noisy fun night aimed at keeping kids off the street. One look at me and she said

"Wow! Sexy lady you look terrific Katie!"

Laughing, I bowed my head and replied. "Well thank you pretty lady" and we both burst into a fit of giggles. We chatted madly all the way as we had a lot to catch up on.

Mark and Theresa were busy planning a future together - she was so in love. I filled her in about school and was asked if I had found myself a boyfriend. My answer was very straight to the point.

"Hell no girl! Not interested in any of the shallow jerks there!"

"Fair enough; maybe you will meet someone tonight." She teased.

She believed everybody should have somebody. She has been a bit of a romantic since meeting Mark. Once we arrived at the church hall I again became uneasy, but at the same time decided I was going to try and have some fun for a change. There was quite a large crowd waiting outside for the doors to open. With my past experience with crowds, I knew it was something I wanted to avoid. Walking the long way never bothered me.

"What's up?" said Theresa once she had parked the car.

"Nothing... Is there a back door?"

"Katie for Christ sake, stop being so bloody stupid! You look fantastic and I'm sure you won't know many of the crowd that comes here. Now let's move it along, and start partying!"

"Oh, I feel sick, I better go home." I said, suddenly feeling faint.

"Katie, just get out of the car. It will be okay I promise." She went on to tell me how both Mark and she would look after me, and no one would cause me grief.

"I promise you are safe with us." Climbing out of the car, I noticed guys watching us and whistling - at Theresa I thought. But then I realised those wolf whistles were for me. I was totally amazed that this fuss was for me! I didn't see many kids from my school, so that was good. The kids that were there, well, none of them bothered me at all. They were all there to have a good time. Theresa and I danced; in between we helped Mark as he was the DJ. He really was a lovely guy; Theresa and Mark made a cute couple. I was enjoying taking requests for the DJ. This was the 1st time I had ever enjoyed a dance, and everything was perfect! A bit like a fairy tale.

With the midnight curfew in place for kids under 18. As the last hour came fast, I was just sitting in the DJ's chair having a drink and watching the kids enjoying their dance moves when a cute boy approached me. I thought I knew him. He was 17 or 18.

"Katie, is that you? I have been watching you for a while now, trying to get up enough courage to come and talk to you - and maybe score a dance. By the way, you look gorgeous!"

"Thank you Steven. It is you right?"
"You remember me then?" He asked.

I reminded him that I had never had the chance to thank him when he rescued me in the playground all those years ago. I had always been too embarrassed to approach him and to be honest I avoided talking to him.

"Well you can say it now by dancing with me." Holding out his hand, he waited for me to place mine in his.

"Nah" I replied.

"You owe me Miss Katie." He laughed.

"Nah I can't dance" was my reply.

"Yes you can I seen you dancing with your friend"

"Ok. Not my fault if you end up with bruised feet and I must warn you I intend to step on your feet!"

"I will take my chances pretty lady" he winked.

The last hour seemed to last forever - we talked some more, danced some more and he even went and got me a drink. The last song was slow and romantic I loved this song by Queen 'Love of my Life'. As he held me close, he smelt so good! He was sweet and so damn handsome. I would remember this moment for the rest of my life.

He gave the impression that he danced to his own tune and ran his own race. I hadn't seen him at school for ages and figured he had left. Either getting a job or maybe he just stayed away from me as I seemed to attract a lot of trouble in those days.

It had been such a wonderful night and now I had so many new and happy things to dream about. We said goodbye, he kissed me and gave me a piece of paper with his phone number; but seriously could I really trust him? I fell asleep thinking of that last dance hoping I would dream sweet things.

Running... It's dark! Something is chasing me. I can hear them breathing. I am not sure if it human or animal. I'm 5 again I'm scared, finding it very hard to breath. I'm trying to scream but there is no sound! I run to a corner sitting cradling my legs rocking back and forth wishing I could become invisible. There is no way out, nowhere to hide! All the sudden I see blood it's all around me I hear screaming yelling I can smell the blood, so much blood. I look down at my hands they are gone, cut off. I see my hands on the floor. I see someone in the shadows. Then I hear the little girl.

"Wake up Katie. Wake up It will be alright, just Wake up."

Waking up from my sleep with the worse headache ever. I looked at my hands they are still attached. Why do I have these nightmares? Why do I feel such pain? I just wanted to be normal - to dream sweet dreams, not dreams of horror. Who was the little girl who wakes me up? Was she real or just a part of my nightmares?

Chapter 17

Felicity

"Hmm" thought the woman in the mirror as she signed into her Facebook page. This guy again. What is with this dude? She checks out his profile again and his photos but she still has no idea who he is. So finally she messages him.

"Hey, I really think you have me mixed up with someone else. I use my married name and no one knows my maiden name except for a few close friends. Sorry but you really do have the wrong person"

"No, I know I have the right woman" he replies and then tells her what her maiden name was.

"Yes absolutely, it is you! I remember you like it was yesterday."

"Good God! That can't be good. They weren't my finest years. I am so sorry but I have no idea who you are. You are obviously a few years older than me." Did she remember him?

She wasn't really sure. That was well over 30 years ago. He sent more information, what year he finished and even what sports he had played. Still nothing...

"I'm truly sorry that was over 30 years ago and really don't remember you" she responded.

Laughing to herself, she posts a new status:

"I HAVE MENOPAUSE AND A TASER GUN"

She laughs at her own cleverness. The woman in the mirror didn't care what people thought of her. She didn't care if she made friends or not. She just liked her privacy. She had found some of the people she knew at school, checking them out, adding only a few and totally ignoring the rest. She never drew attention to herself or what she did. It was her secret and hers alone. She often joked with her few friends how unsexy she was and how she had passed her 'used by date'. She often wondered what some of their reactions would be if they knew of Felicity. But the thought of it would just make her crack up with uncontrollable laughter.

"ME? A private sexy dancer? Perish the thought!" She truly had never been tempted to reveal herself to anyone, even her closest friend. She had to keep this to herself. It was the one thing that was hers, for better or worse. She was after all FELICITY.

She knew they would misjudge her. Or was it her who would be the one misjudging them? Without giving them the slightest chance to have any form of opinion. She had feelings of wanting to be totally alone, shutting the world out completely. She would often lie, telling friends she would not be home when they would ring to say they were coming over. She didn't really worry about her declining lists of friends as this had been her life choice.

Although a friend - once in a while, would have been nice to talk and share things with. She really believed she was happy this way. It was less stressful for her as friends were hard work. Always having to be on her guard; being careful not to offend them. One friend, whom she had let get to know her more so than the others, would just show up without calling.

"Well if I ring you, you'll just put me off." was her reasoning. "And besides, what can you do once I am here?"

Well the woman in the mirror had to agree with her, she was indeed very right as she would have made up some excuse.

'Lights, camera, action!' Viewers began clocking on her cam before she even turned it on and already is up to 300 and climbing fast. Messages are flooding the screen, people eager to see her. The music starts and her cam goes on. Felicity is simply breathtaking, no matter what she wears!

Queen's 'Fat Bottom Girls' is playing loudly in the background.

She looks like a biker chick done Felicity's way. Moving to the beat of the throbbing music, she is dressed in vinyl thigh high boots, with large silver buckles and tiny black leather shorts that tie up in the front with black laces. A cute little bra type jacket, short and sassy, completes this part of the ensemble. One of her best, she is sure. Her wig is a very curly, long dark brown. Already 900 viewers and they haven't seen anything yet! But within a few seconds, 1,200 viewers are clogging up the web as she begins her sensuous dance moves, every one of them aimed to leave them wanting more.

Looking at her messages filling the screen, she continues to dance, moving with such purpose. She knows all eyes are on her:

'MARRY ME FELICITY'

'$25000 FOR ONE NIGHT WITH YOU'

'I WISH MY GIRLFRIEND LOOKED AS HOT AS YOU'

She dances around laughing and while doing so - slowly removes her jacket with such class and sophistication. Of course her black leather and lace lingerie is perfect. Then all of a sudden a horror hits her.

Oh my god! Was the guy on Facebook one of her fans? How the hell did that happen? No he couldn't be, he was from school and besides she was always so careful to hide her identity.

She thought. "No one could find me. I am always so careful!"

She is jolted back to reality when the phone rings with a text message. She looks at her phone message and goes as white as a ghost:

'I KNOW WHO YOU ARE, WHY DON'T YOU REMEMBER ME?'

She drops the phone in terror and turns off the camera.

"My god, after all this time someone has found out my deepest, innermost secret!" The woman in the mirror is not so confident now. Who is this guy? All her fears come rushing back. Is it some horrible twist of fate? Was the guy on Facebook and the one sending the phone texts, the same person?

"Fuck what do I do now?" She asked herself. Her first reaction is to remove her mobile number from her profile information. Again she wonders how he traced her. The profile of 'Felicity' is nothing like her Facebook page. She then signs back into her Facebook account and there is another message from the man.
'DANCE WITH ME.'

"Oh my god! He does know I am Felicity." she screams aloud, as she sends him a message. "Leave me alone! You have the wrong person!"

Trying to remain calm, she runs to her bar and pours herself a very large glass of wine and lights cigarette. Shaking uncontrollably, she doesn't know what to do. Whom can she tell? No one. She has no one she can tell. She has distanced herself from any close relationships over the years so there is no one she can tell her secret too.

She goes back to her cam web site account and there are hundreds of messages from people wondering where she went in such a hurry. She looks to see if there is any hint of who he may be on Felicity's site. Is the guy on Facebook a member on her site? Deciding she was over reacting she turns her cam back on and straight away the viewer's clock on fast and messages start to flood her screen. She blows a kiss, waves and starts her show again.

Chapter 18

Katie

Nightmare after nightmare; No two are ever the same. Each one is just a little scarier and horrifying than the one before. I am always 5 or 6. Sometimes I see Mum and other times, just me. I never see my father, Kyle or Lorna. The fainting spells, built up anger and the total lack of trust in myself or anyone else became worse. So many emotions I just couldn't handle.

It is so overwhelming not being able to tell the difference between nightmares and reality. The only positive thing was that school was going at a more tolerable pace now. The kids left me alone and I was now able to wear small amounts of makeup and pretty clothes - which I loved to show off mainly around the house because I didn't like to go out. I was not too keen on all the new attention I was attracting; but at least it was positive and no longer negative or nasty.

Theresa rang me the day after the disco.

"Who was the spunk you were dancing with last night?"

"Oh for goodness sake, two dances Theresa! Hardly a Romeo and Juliet romance!" Smiling as I was quite smitten with him. I explained who Steven was and how he was the boy who had rescued me that day at school.

"Remember when that can accidently threw itself at my head?" I laughed rather nervously.

"Did he ask you out?"

"Nope, we simply said goodnight." I replied that he gave me his number.

"So that explains why we found you hiding in the car. You have to ring him Katie!" she giggled.

"Maybe I will, maybe I won't" I said teasing her.

"Katie, He seemed so nice and reallllllllly handsome."

"Yeah he was a spunk, hey and so sweet" I answered, still daydreaming of our last dance together.

"No I am just not interested, and no I am not a lesbian." I laughed snapping back to reality. She laughed so hard at my lame and uncalled for comment.

"Maybe I will go to the next dance and see if he turns up. Will that make you happy Theresa?"

"You go, Katie girl! The church is going to hold the discos once a month now as last night's was such a success... The church - who likes to raise all the money they can, has agreed to them being a monthly event" She added that Mark would continue in his role as DJ.

"Oh great" I said laughing. "All a girl needs is another monthly pain" I said goodbye and hung up still smiling. I really liked Theresa, even with her over the top romantic notions.

My life was easing up; Dad was away more often now than he was home. Kyle and Lorna were growing up fast and I loved how happy Mum was when he wasn't around. She loved her job at the local hospital.

One afternoon in March, as I got off the high school bus and waited for Lorna and Kyle's bus, I saw the Military Police drive down our street. I wondered what had happened but quickly pushed it out of my mind as the bus arrived with The Munchkins. Kyle was always a happy child nothing seemed to bother him while Lorna always seemed to be in her own world. Walking home, Lorna was chatting away to one of her imaginary friends.

"Who are you chatting to Munchkin?" I asked her.

"Well Dad of course silly." Kyle over-hearing her, turned around.

"Good! Tell him I said he's a bloody dickhead and that I hate him!" I tried not to laugh and reminded him that was neither nice nor funny.

"Well, who cares?" He answered quickly. Lorna looked at us. Almost in a serious and in a sad way she said very softly

"Dad says he is sorry."

"Lorna I love you Munchkin, but there is no one here just you me and Kyle."

"No wonder all the kids at schools think she is a Looney Toon!" was Kyle's cheeky reply.

"I don't care what any of you think! I'm telling the truth, I swear I am, Katie!"

"It's ok Munchkin I believe you and so does Kyle" clipping him across the head.

"Yeah ok I believe ya... ya happy now Miss bossy boots Katie"

"Just try and be nice Kyle okay" as I reminded them we needed to walk a lot faster as Kyle had to get ready for cricket practice.

As we got closer, I could see that the Military's Police cars were at our house. I began to fear the worst, thinking all sorts of awful things. We all ran as fast as we could.

"Shit! What are the police doing at our house?" was Kyle's comment.

"What is wrong with you today?" I scolded. "Watch your language"

"I have been trying to tell you both!" Lorna yelled.

But we didn't answer - picking up the pace we ran even faster and as we entered the house, two Military Police where there with mum. One was sitting next to her.

"Mum what is wrong?" We all yelled at once. Mum looked up, but I don't think she even saw us.

With tears streaming down her face she said in a barely audible soft voice.

"Your Dad was killed in an accident today. His car was hit by a truck and he died instantly."

"They tell me he did not suffer at all." She added, as if, to try and make it easier for us and perhaps herself.

"Oh my god!" Was all I could manage; and Kyle had disappeared into his room. Lorna just hugged our mother - trying to tell her that Dad had come to school to say sorry and goodbye. But no words were reaching our Mum. She just sat silent. Why did I feel relief instead of sorrow? Why didn't I care? He was my father. Shouldn't I be crying or feeling some kind of remorse? After the Military Police had left Mum was incredibly strong, though not as sad as a wife should be of such news. Maybe it was the shock, but it was like a huge heavy weight had been lifted off her often sad shoulders. Maybe now she was free? As if she was reading my mind, she turned and said calmly

"It will be ok Katie. We have 2 weeks to move out of the house and the Army village."

"And then what do we do?" I asked.

"It is okay sweetie. I have been saving some money every payday for the past 5 years. By adding some more from the housekeeping money your Dad gave me over the past 15 years, we have a tidy sum saved up."

With that she went to her room and came back with a bank book. Handing it to me I could not believe my eyes! Mum had managed to save $39,543.

"How?" I asked.

"A little here and there." She went on to explain that she had an idea Dad kind of knew, but she had it in her own name and very well hidden.

"It was for a rainy day in case of an emergency Katie."

The funeral was to be taken care of by the Army and he would be buried with full military honours. Of course they won't help us find somewhere to live or even help with the move.

In Mum's words "We are on our own."

I didn't see then how hard this must have been for her or how she was going to do it on her own with just me and the two Munchkins. As if she knew my every thought, she turned to me and said

"I am not sure how we will manage, but I have rung your uncle and he will be flying in on Thursday. He will know what to do. He will help us... Smile it is going to be alright. I will have to work, but I will have you. You're such a great help. You are my rock, Katie! I have always been able to count on you."

I tried to explain that I could leave school and get a job to help.

"No, you finish year 10 first love. Promise me. And you will be helping by watching over Kyle and Lorna."

I went to console my brother, who was very quiet and withdrawn. "Hey hairy legs, how are you doing?"

"Just go away! I don't want to talk to nobody!" Touching his cheek, I simply said

"Ok sweetie you know where I am if you need me."

"Katie I didn't mean the awful things I said about Dad."

"It's okay Munchkin I know. I'm sure Dad would forgive you" hugging him and leaving him alone.

As I passed Lorna's door it was closed. I listened closely through the door and could hear her in deep conversation with someone.

"Why did you leave? Didn't you like us? And why am I the only one who can see you?" thinking this was just the way an eight year old handles her grief, I knocked then entered.

"Hey Munchkin, how are you doing?"

"Oh I am fine Katie." She said smiling. "I was just talking to Daddy. He says he is very sorry. And that he really did love us all."

"Lorna sweetheart, Dad died today. He isn't here."

"Yes Katie, I know that. I tried to tell you on the way home from school. He turned up at school today just before the bus came."

"What?" I said utterly dumbfounded.

"Katie I see him he is standing right here." Pointing to her left.

"Lorna you have to stop talking to yourself like this. It will break Mums heart". She answered me very plainly.

"I do not talk to myself and I am not silly like all the kids at school think." And with indignation, she added "So there!"

"I am sorry Munchkin but I only see you standing here in front of me."

Getting more upset she cried "I do see him Katie! Why won't anyone believe me? I am not crazy!"

To try and stop her being so upset, I calmly said "Lorna, I do believe you but let's just keep it to ourselves. We don't want to hurt mummy any more do we? And, tell Dad I accept his apology but I will never forgive him."

"Dad says he wishes he could change things." Lorna said softly.

I replied that it was too little too late and then I left her to be in her own little world, where ever that was. Lorna really was one of a kind, a special little girl.

Finally falling asleep, I drift in and out of slumber. I see my Mum. She is happy and laughing. But a man is running towards her!

"Run Mum!" I scream. "Run!" She looks up but isn't scared.

"No, I am not running." She answers.

He is hurting her - punching her, she doesn't cry she just gets up and try's to walk away... Mum sees me she starts to wave she tells me to run away. Then he pulls a gun out shoots her right through the heart.

"Mum oh my god. Mums please don't die. I need you." Crying, trying so hard to reach her. Why can't I help her? Then I hear the little girl.

"Wake up Katie. Wake up! It will be alright, just wake up."

Jolting awake in a hot sweat; I run to check on Mum and the Munchkins. They're sound asleep. Mum looks worn out yet so peaceful, so I lock my door and climb out my window grabbing my box from under the house. I slowly have a drink and light a cigarette, I decide to go for one of my midnight walks and try to clear my head and make sense of my nightmares and the awful day...

Chapter 19

Katie

Dad's funeral was today. It was a full on military event. Many soldiers saying kind words about how he was just such a good guy. Words I knew to be untrue. None of them knew him like we did. None of them knew the real man. Mum was somehow different. More in control and grounded than I had ever seen her. Our Uncle helped us get through the day and later he helped us find a place to rent for a few months - just while we waited for a unit Mum was planning on buying. It was near the hospital, so she could go back to work full-time.

Kyle became his normal obnoxious self again with his happy go lucky attitude, finding lots of ways to amuse himself and sometimes us to. Things were slowly coming together. The last few weeks had been hectic but we had each other to hold onto. Lorna - on the other hand seemed to become more isolated, preferring her own company even more now than before Dad's death. I found a part time job for Thursday nights and Saturday mornings. The money I made went into a bank account until I decided what I wanted to do with my future. My nightmares were still the same, as were my drinking binges and midnight walks. I enjoyed my solitude. The night was a calm place for me, at least when I was awake.

We finally moved to a 3 bedroom unit in Liverpool - just a few minutes' walk from the hospital where Mum was working. I was able to continue at my current school by catching the bus. Mum transferred Kyle and Lorna to the local school, which was also only a short walk away. I was nearly 17 and had so much responsibility for a girl so young.

Mum worked a lot; she also started going out with her girlfriends from work more and more on a regular basis - coming home in the early hours of the morning. I had to take control of most of the daily chores and even went to parent teachers' nights for the kids. Most parents at the new school thought I was their mother. We started to see less of Mum. It was as if she was the teenager and I was the adult.

Then Mum started dating which I felt was odd as Dad had only been gone a few months. In any case my midnight drinking and walks were easier now. Mum - it seems - didn't want to know or didn't care, and because she didn't drive I had to catch the train to work and home on Thursday nights. I wasn't scared or worried I would just read my book becoming intrigued with the story. One night while reading a really good book, I missed my station. The station I got off at was un-manned; and of course the phone at the station was broken, I had no way of reaching Mum so I started to walk towards home. Not seeing or noticing any of the people or cars I continued to walk.

I must have walked for nearly an hour or it at least felt like it, I had forgotten my watch. I finally went around the corner of the long street we lived in when suddenly I had the eeriest feeling, and could feel my blood run cold. I felt someone was trying to tell me something. By now I was getting really scared. I know I was only a few streets away from our unit so I started to walk faster. Suddenly a car stops; a man jumps out and grabs me forcing me into the car. Pushing me into the back seat, I couldn't scream or see outside. Punching me in the face so hard I feel like my jaw has broken. I tried to scream but they just kept punching me, calling me awful names. This was my nightmare but I was awake. OH MY GOD! Wake up Katie Oh My God! This is really happening it's not a nightmare. Please someone help me! I just know I'm going to die. As I was thrown into the back seat I seen there was 3 more men. Two of them held me down with such a force that I'm sure my ribs broke. I could not see out of the car. Then I heard the little girl - I can feel her touching my hand.

"Katie, it will be alright! Close your eyes and remember every direction you take!" One man had a knife to my throat. I could smell my own blood and feel my tears streaming down my face.

I knew the little girl was with me; I could feel her. Why did she haunt my dreams? Had my nightmares all these years been a warning? What did she want? What did she know? - I can't breathe his hands are too tight around my throat. Then everything goes blank all of the sudden, I'm floating above my body. I'm not scared; I see her she is holding my hand tightly. I look at her; she is so young, so beautiful.

"Am I dead?" I asked her.

"No Katie. Be strong, everything will be okay"

"Please don't leave me!" I pleaded.

"I am always with you Katie. I will never leave you."

"I'm scared I'm going to die aren't I?"

"No Katie, please be strong. Try and remember everything you can - every detail of the journey"

Then back to my living nightmare - the smell of blood and the pain of broken bones. I lay still but my eyes were open. I focused on the trees, buildings and street signs that I could see; remembering every turn the car took.

The car stopped and I could see we were in a car park under a block of units. As they dragged me up the stairs, I counted every one. I managed to see the number on the door to the apartment. I punched and kicked with all my might, but they just beat me more. I was then thrown into a room and the door was locked. I heard loud music and laughing - I knew they were drinking.

Oh my God! My Mum will be frantic! She won't be able to find me! Who will care for my family? They just lost Dad, they can't lose me too. My brain was a scrambled mess. I went to the windows but they were nailed shut. I can see - from the street light, the colours of houses, units and cars. I swear I am on the second floor. I started screaming!

"Wake up Katie! Wake up!" But this was no nightmare. This was real. I heard the door unlock and two of the men entered. My nightmare had begun.

"Please let me go!" I begged.

"Shut up you fucking bitch. You are going nowhere!"

Oh my god, I was in a living nightmare... Then one of the men held me down and covered my face with a cloth - which they soaked with something from a brown bottle. I try to fight but they are so much bigger and stronger than me. I just give up fighting and fall to the floor, I feel my head hit the ground so hard...I'm sure my life is over.

Chapter 20

Melinda's Story

It has been nearly 30 years since Melinda's death. Her young friend Phyllis is now a grown woman with children of her own. Sitting by Melinda's grave - as she often did when she came back to the town to visit. Chatting away about anything and everything, positive that Melinda hears her every word...

"Hello Phyllis! I heard you were back in town for a visit." Turning around quickly with a shock, she sees an old man in his late eighties.

"Hi" she manages to say.

"Mr Booth, is that you?"

"Yes Phyllis. How have you been? My goodness you have grown into a lovely young woman" he replied.

"Thank you... and yes it's been nearly 20 odd years and well I'm... I'm a mum now." Puzzled, she looks at the flowers in his hand.

"Are you here visiting someone?"

"Melinda" he said.

"I promised Mable years ago I would look after Melinda's grave for as long as I was able." After a second he added. "But I'm not getting any younger or any better looking" He was laughing at his own words.

"Whatever happened to Mable?" Phyllis asked.

"There was a rumour she had passed away a few years after Melinda died; she left town and no one knew or heard anything about her... She was heartbroken and so lost without her Melinda." replied Mr Booth.

"Oh, so that explains why Melinda's grave is so well looked after. You bring her flowers all the time?" Phyllis asked.

"Sure do!" he smiled. "Every month for the past 30 years. Daisies... She loved Daisies" Mr Booth added.

"That's really nice of you Mr Booth - very sweet and thoughtful. Yes Melinda loved daisies" Phyllis added.

"I still miss her; even now to this day I can't believe she is gone. She missed out on so much - dying so young. She never had a chance to live a full life... She was special, you know? One of kind" All the sudden Mr Booth burst into tears.

"Mr Booth! I'm sorry! Did I say something to upset you? I'm so sorry if I did." Phyllis said putting her arms around the old man.

"No Phyllis, it wasn't you. Look, I'm an old man with not long on this earth. I need to make things right before I go, make peace with my maker" he said.

"What?" Phyllis asked as she looked up. She thought she seen Melinda over near the trees, waving and pulling funny faces at her.

"Oh! My! God! You know what happened to Melinda, don't you?" Phyllis demanded an answer. "I want to know! I need to know!"

"Yes. It's time I told the story. I actually came looking for you when I heard you were in town." He said as he slowly climbed down to sit on the ground.

"I have already been to the police and lodged my statement this morning. I'm a dreadful man - if Mable had known the truth she might have been able to get over Melinda's death." Mr Booth sat there with his head down...

"Mable would never have gotten over Melinda's death!" screamed Phyllis with a building anger. "What did you do?"

"I remember that day like it was yesterday." He spoke like he was in a trance.

"I was just about to drive home from town when I saw Melinda running towards the creek. My grandson was chasing her, throwing stones and calling her names." He said, now crying like a baby.

"I jumped out of the car and chased them, I called out to Tommy but he didn't hear me. By the time I caught up, Melinda was crying and pleading with him to leave her alone. Tommy was shoving and pushing her, and taunting her with names. I yelled out for him to stop. He heard me, turning around as he did; Melinda looked up through her tears. When she saw me, she turned to run - tripping over, she fell and hit her head hard on a rock."

"But I swear she was alive! I asked her if she was alright and she said yes. I grabbed Tommy by the shirt, dragging him away to my truck. I was so ashamed of my grandson, treating another human like that especially a little girl... It's my fault I shouldn't have left her." He was sobbing, almost uncontrollably.

"I didn't know about her death until that next morning and I was so ashamed with what Tommy did... but you must understand I couldn't go to the police! He didn't kill her! I swear she tripped! But I do know it wouldn't have happened if he wasn't taunting and chasing her. He was only young! I didn't want him to go to jail. It wouldn't have brought Melinda back" Phyllis was standing there in shock at Mr Booth's confession.

"Melinda was only thirteen! She was young too! She didn't deserve to die like that." Phyllis screamed.

"Where is Tommy now?" she demanded.

"Tommy killed himself four years later, just before his eighteenth birthday. I guess the guilt became too much for him to bare." Mr Booth sobbed. As if this made what he had said any better.

All of a sudden her legs had given way and Phyllis was sitting on the ground, looking almost like a child lost with nowhere to go...

"Why tell me this now?" she asked, sobbing. "Why the hell now? You should have told Mable this, years ago... Told the police... Taken Melinda home... Oh my God! My poor Melinda! She must have been so scared! She died all alone" Phyllis yelled through her tears.

As Phyllis looked up at her friend's grave, she swears she could see Melinda standing there. Smiling, blowing a kiss and nodding with a look on her face that said it was okay she didn't blame anyone. Phyllis knew in her heart Melinda had forgiven both Mr Booth and Tommy. Mr Booth was an old man now and it wasn't his crime to pay for. Tommy was gone from his own hand so he had paid a very high price - the guilt of that awful day being too much for him to bear. Mr Booth had lived with this evil secret for long enough, he deserved to die peacefully.

Phyllis found peace in knowing the truth of that dreadful day almost 30 years ago. Knowing all this could never bring Melinda back or make her death easier to understand. But holding an old man accountable for his grandson's actions was silly and he had lost his only grandson in a twist of fate. Holding Mr Booths hands; looking at him, Phyllis speaks ever so softly.

"Thank you, Mr Booth for telling me the truth. I'm sure in her heart Melinda forgives you. It wasn't your fault by any means."

"I'm so sorry Phyllis... for everything"

"I think you have suffered enough guilt Mr Booth." Phyllis says offering a hug.

"I'm sure Melinda would forgive you both and wish you well. You see, Melinda was a special Person - even though she suffered so much, and lived through so much bullying and negativity from people. She wouldn't have hurt another person ever. She taught me so much, even though she was so young and yes... robbed of her life. I'm just so glad I had the chance to know her, even if it was for such a short time."

Phyllis turns back to her friend's grave and says

"Fly back to me Melinda! I will love you forever! Thank you for being my friend!"

Mr Booth died a few months later. Phyllis attended his funeral and thought he looked peaceful. She laid daisies on the dirt of his final resting place and left him a set of Angel wings.

"Have a wonderful time in heaven Mr Booth, we shall meet again. Save me a seat"

She was sure her young friend was there that day, she could feel her. Phyllis smiled to herself, she knew Melinda was there to take Mr Booth's hand and guide him to heaven. She just knew Melinda was an Angel in heaven as she was an Angel here on earth...

Chapter 21

Katie

Another nightmare... I am 5 again... I'm running and I hear gunshots, I'm in the bush and it is very dark, I'm scared, I can hear dogs barking loudly, I see blood, so much blood! I find a hole and jump in to hide. Oh god, it is a GRAVE! Dirt slowly begins filling the hole. It's a grave... oh my god it's my grave. I see my tombstone; then all of a sudden I'm in a coffin. I can hear the dirt falling onto the box.

"STOP PLEASE STOP IM NOT DEAD STOP"

Then I hear the little girl.

"Wake up Katie. Wake up. It will be alright, just wake up."

I try to open my eyes but they hurt. My whole body is in pain. Where I am is dark, but I see a little light. I feel around, I seem to be in a plastic bag. After what seems like a lifetime, I manage to break through the bag with what strength I have. At first I cannot stand. I'm so sore. There is pain everywhere and I'm covered in dry blood. I seem to be near a creek. I scream for help but no one answers.

"Help! Help!" I scream for what seems like a lifetime. It looks like I am under a bridge.

"God, what day is it? Where am I?" the memories of what happened flooding back to me.

"What time is it?" I try to run but I can barely walk. My eyes sting; the daylight is blinding me.

"Are those men following me to finish the job?" I start to panic.

Somehow I find a road. I can see a phone box. In the glass of the phone box I can see my reflection. Shit! I didn't even recognize who that person was. There is no sign of me, in the reflection. I don't know the girl looking back at me. I am covered in blood... My once pretty dress is torn and covered with blood stains. My shoes and bag is missing, along with my all of my ID.

"What if they have gone after my family?" I dial triple zero immediately. I can barely hear the voice on the other end.

"Police? Please, help me!" I am almost whispering because I am so weak and scared they might hear me. Then I hear a kind voice ask where I am.

"I don't know" I replied.

"Look for a street sign sweetie. It will be ok, just take your time."

"Yes! Yes! I can see a sign." Giving him the name of the street; I remember falling then everything went dark. It was like I was falling into a deep pit. Was there a way out this time?

"Hi there Sweetie, you are safe now." I hear a sweet voice.

I look up to see a young police woman looking at me and holding my hand.

"You are safe now."

"Where am I?"

"You're in the hospital. Do you know what happened?"

"Where is my mother? I have to call my mother please!" I almost screamed. "What day is it?" The questions just shot out of my mouth. It was like I had to get everything out at once, just in case the nightmare began again. Slowly and softly the police woman answered all my questions, telling me it was Monday.

"But that can't be right! It was Thursday when I was walking home."

"Are you Katie Green?" her response.

"Yes, Yes I am"

"Well, your mum is here and you can see her soon. She had you listed as a missing person since that night. She and the rest of us thought we had lost you. We are all so glad to have found you alive!"

"Am I really alive?" I said with tears streaming down my face. "Why do I feel so dead?" I slurred as I drifted back off to sleep.

As I started to wake up, I heard my Mum come in the door. She screamed when she saw me.

"Please Mum! It is okay. Please don't cry!" she explained how she had been out searching the streets. How she even had the taxi and hospital staff out looking too. She said Kyle had helped so much... He just would not stop. He barely slept or ate.

"But he is only 11!" I said.

"Katie, we thought we had lost you forever!" I wanted to see Lorna and Kyle.

Finally they were allowed in. After I assured everyone; including myself that I could handle it.

"I have already been to hell and back. I need to see my two Munchkins."

I kept crying most of that day; and was reassured that none of this had been my fault. Mum and the police assured me they would get these men. They were certain these men had done this before but had never been able to get a good description of them.

There were so many medical tests, so many questions. It was so draining... I just wanted to sleep! Although it sounds stupid now, I sometimes didn't want to wake up. I had no idea what further nightmares lay ahead of me. Then when I become more alert, a kind and large policeman - "Zorba" I nicknamed him - came into the room.

"Katie we need a statement. It won't be nice, or easy. But we have to know so we can put these bastards away!" I think I smiled, as I never imagined a policeman would swear. The nice policewoman was there as well. Mum told me to be brave and truthful and to tell them everything they needed to know. She would be right outside the door and she told me that I was the bravest young woman she knew!

Lorna, Mum and Kyle all chorused "We love you!" Kyle winked and added his usual melt your heart smile.

I finally felt a little safer. A few hours later, after routine testing, I was discharged from the hospital. I was classified as a rape victim. I started to blame myself completely. Why did I walk home by myself...? Everything was now becoming so real and so much clearer. I had been the victim... I finally felt in control of my destiny. I had survived and was able to relay every detail of it all to the police. Then the questions started again. Three more detectives entered the room.

"Katie, we have tried so hard to find you - you are such a brave, brave girl and we need you to remain brave." Was all they could say.

"Katie, do you know where they took you?"

I told them no, but if we returned to where I was first snatched - I was sure I could direct them. They told my mother someone could take her and the kids' home; but Kyle, Lorna and her all refused to budge. They chose to wait right at the police station for me.

"We're never going to lose you again!" was my mother's response.

So with several detectives in one car and 2 other cars full of policemen, we started off to where I had been snatched. I cannot... for the life of me, tell you how I did it, it was like a voice in my head. I climbed into the back seat of the car and laid down, looking around from the same position I was forced into that night. I remembered every direction the car had travelled that near fatal night. I was now well aware, along with the police that I had been indeed left to die! Suddenly I sat up. I had recognised the ceiling of the underground car park the police car was driving into. Jumping out of the car, I yelled.

"There!" I said pointing to one of the units.

As I started walking towards the stairs the police held me back. They continued on from my directions. I kept screaming "The second floor! The second door!"

At this stage a kind detective instructed the two young police women to take me to the car. As I sat there, the men were dragged out in handcuffs and thrown into the paddy wagon. I recognised every one of their faces - they will be forever etched in my memory until I die!

"Well done Katie! We got them and we also found your bag, some of your clothing and your ID in the room. They had made no attempt to hide anything, not even the solution they had used to knock you unconscious."

I was later to learn that along with samples of my blood, body and hair tissues. They had also found the type of tape they had used to gag me, and of course the same type of plastic bag they put me in when they threw me out of the car like garbage. On closer examination of their car, there was a large ding on the front end where I said I was sure they had hit something.

Soon there were police cars everywhere. The forensic teams took over the block of units. Every part of the car park was taped off to the public. God! Was my nightmare ending or was it only just starting? I knew that what lay ahead of me would not be easy, but I survived and I knew I had to fight and this time I would win!

"Where was my little girl?" Was she still here? I knew she was. I could feel her around me.

My nightmare was only just beginning. I had to pick them out in four separate line-ups and I had to be fingerprinted so they could match my fingerprints to those found in the unit - to prove I had been there. The main culprit, the most evil person I had ever seen or will ever see again in this lifetime, yelled out at me.

"I will get you! You are dead! You are lying, you bitch!"

The men were charged immediately and held without bail.

"I am not lying!" I told the detectives over and over again.

"We know Katie, and the charges will go ahead. It will not be easy, but we will be here for you every step of the way. You are one hell of an incredible young lady and you have survived for a reason. We have to get this scum off the street. So no other young woman has to ever suffer or die by their hands."

By this stage I had been awake for over 36 hours. I was so tired that I honestly felt I was going crazy. I was happily talking to the little girl when Mum met me at the police station.

"Katie darling, who are you talking to?"

"Her." I said turning around to see no-one there. Bursting into tears I screamed "I'm going crazy aren't I?"

"No sweetie, you are not!" was my mother's gentle reply. "We all love you darling and are so grateful to have you back. We will face this together."

I kept repeating over and over again how sorry I was. But both Mum and the police told me that I was the victim and that all the men responsible will be punished.

Chapter 22

Felicity

Lights, camera, action! Felicity enters the room with a style and class of her own. She demands everyone's attention as only she can. With the music roaring loudly, 'I am Woman', she is standing there facing the cam. Her costume is cheeky and classy all rolled into one. Her light brown wig is short with wild out of control curls. Round yellow sunglasses are hiding her eyes and trademark bright nails and lipstick. Dancing around so classy and sexy her viewers are clocking up quickly. 588 so far. A long sleeve yellow shirt - tied up loosely above her belly button. A short yellow tutu that flutters and swings around from her movements; when she turns you can see a lion's tail. Yellow stockings and a pair of brown high ankle boots cover her feet. Felicity's costume is a cheeky lion done her way...

'I am Woman! Hear me roar!' The musical notes float loudly from her sound system. Messages start coming through at a rapid rate, from men trying to attract her attention. But all she does is smile blow a kiss and wave.

'MARRY ME'

'I WANT YOU'

'TALK TO ME'

'I WILL GIVE YOU ANYTHING YOU WANT'

'Anything I want?' She thinks 'I have everything I want. I don't need anyone. I like my life as it is.' Dancing, moving around to the beat and removing her shirt gets the views up to 1690... All eyes on her!

'IM WEATHY I CAN LOOK AFTER YOU'

'Big deal. I can look after myself.' she thinks. So many messages now flooding her screen! Dropping her shirt, she smiles and spins round.

Felicity knows she has everyone's attention but she doesn't need anyone...

'OH MY GOD'

'CHAT TO ME'

So many messages and she replies to none. Off comes the tutu to reveal her lingerie. Standing there, facing the cam, she is an all-natural Woman! She is Felicity! Her lingerie is a soft yellow, resting perfectly on her figure, showing her curves and hiding her imperfections. She takes off her bra and covers her chest with her hands. Turning around, she removes her briefs. Spinning back round to the cam she uncovers her breasts, she blows a kiss, wave's goodbye and turns off the cam.

She takes off her wig and washes off the makeup. The woman in the mirror has returned.

'Good grief!' she thinks, coming out of the bathroom in her PJ's. 'So many viewers tonight... More than usual... Not bad for a middle aged woman!' Jumping back on the computer and going to her Facebook page - where no one knows about Felicity. She looks for her best mate, a guy in Canada. They met in chat room seven years ago. She likes chat rooms. She gets the human interaction she needs without having to meet people in person. It's her sanctuary. She feels safe. She can be anyone she wants.

Her Canadian friend understands her as she understands him. Together, they share things. They never judge each other, and are always there for each other. He's a person whom she has never met. He doesn't know about her double life and she seriously doesn't think he would care. They have something in common. They both have Bipolar. Bipolar isn't a bad word. It doesn't mean they're insane. It's a chemical imbalance, usually triggered by some event or maybe something that has happened in the past. You can't tell who has it unless they tell you. And usually when you say you have it, people seem to run away. He is the perfect friend; a 'girlfriend' - without the raging hormones or mood swings.

'If he shits me, I can pull the plug.' She thinks to herself, laughing out loud.

She has found a few close friends via the internet, including a very special lady from Canada whom she loves to pieces and a few new friends - Americans, New Zealanders and quite a few Australians. It's amazing who you can you meet online and get close to, even if you have never met them in person. They are friends who don't judge her and love her for who she is.

Sometimes it seems it's just better to talk to someone who you can't see... Then she notices another message from that guy.

'Come dance with me! I don't care if you step on my feet!'

'What the fuck! Why doesn't he give up?' She thinks to herself.

"Go away!" She sends back to him. She's at the end of her patients with him. She decides it's time to post a new status on her Facebook page.

"Granny knickers and hipster jeans are sexy, damn it!"

'Pretty clever...' She thought. Laughing to herself, she shuts down the computer.

The next morning the doorbell rings and she goes to see who it is. A florist, with a large bunch of flowers! She accepts the flowers and goes inside. Such beautiful flowers they are. Purple Iris's with white and pink Roses mixed in. Pulling out the card, she reads:

"Come dance with me! Please meet me at the corner Café at 3pm tomorrow."

A sinking feeling comes over her, someone knows her secret. 'That's it! I have had enough! I will go and sort this out once and for all!' she thinks.

Crawling into bed she dreams of a place where everything is easy and worries don't happen.

Chapter 23

Katie

Nightmares again; creeping into my sleep. It is dark, cold and raining. I am alone and just waking up.

"Katie, Katie wake up" it was little Lorna.

"Hey Munchkin, what's up?" I am now more awake.

"She said you will be okay now"

"Oh that's good." I replied feeling very puzzled.

"Who?" was my next response.

"The little girl, she is telling me it will all be OK."

"Good" I said. "Have you got a new friend?"

"Nope... She is your angel." Was Lorna's quirky reply.

First I almost lost the power to speak. "I have an angel?"

"Of course silly...! She has been sitting here all night watching over you"

I will never be able to explain my following thoughts - but I felt so at peace, so serene. I felt like an invisible shield of protection had gone up around me.

"Should I be scared?" I asked laughing.

"Oh Katie, don't be so silly. She loves you and watches over you"

"You are one weird kid!" I gently patted Lorna on the head.

"I already know that, tell me something I don't know" She said, skipping out of the room chatting happily to herself.

She was one of a kind. I was so glad she was our one of a kind. Now to try and catch some much needed sleep. As I closed my eyes, Kyle's head came around the door frame.

"Wake up sleepy head!" he yelled.

"And a good morning to you too hairy legs!" I waved for him to come in closer to me.

Bursting into tears, he cried. "Katie, I am so sorry! I tried so hard to find you! I looked everywhere I thought you might be and even places I didn't think you were. I just looked everywhere! I had to find you Katie" he kept crying. Holding him close to me I told him

"Kyle, sweetie, I do know how hard you tried to find me. Please don't cry. I am home with everyone now and that makes me glad to be back. Little guy, don't you ever forget how much I love you."

"I am going to be big soon and when I am I will always be here to protect you. I promise." He then chimed in with "You are still the prettiest girl I know!"

"Just know and believe this Munchkin, I will never leave you again. Okay?!" I said grabbing him and tickling his ribs until the tears of sadness became those of happiness.

A few days later my head was still a blur. My body continued to ache but with a little less enthusiasm. Looking in the mirror now since that first time on that awful night - I felt I was starting to see past the black eyes, busted nose, split swollen lips and even the 6 stitches above my eye. But the real scars I have been permanently marked with would never be seen. They would be with me for eternity. Then I realised that I wasn't meant to be here, alive. But I was. I had survived this ordeal; battered and scarred, but I was ALIVE!

Now with the help of the police, my barrister, the rape crisis councillor and my Mum, I was about to go through the worst nightmare of my life. I was able to enter the justice system and face not only the four accused, but each of their barristers. I felt I had no choice, but I will be strong. I knew how I would be treated - being accused of going willingly. But the worse thought was if I didn't, who would be their next victim? I still remember they had seen my ID and could send their friends after my family. My real fear was that the next girl they snatched would die at their hands... I know I was not meant to wake up in that plastic bag. I was meant to suffocate. Maybe the drug they used to render me unconscious wore off too fast? Thank god for my little girl waking me up. Was she there or was it just my mind playing tricks? Why were bad things happening to me when I just started to get my life in order? Suddenly Mum knocked on my door. "Katie your friends are here. Is it okay for them to come in?"

"Oh my God! Did you tell them?"
" Sweetie you have to understand, we were searching for you and rang everyone we could think of."

"No! I do not want them to see me!" The girls were only outside the door and could hear the conversation. Linda popped her head around the corner.

"Katie, please!" She said walking into the room.

"We just need to see you and know you are alive" Nicole took one look at me and burst into tears, hugging me so tight I could barely breathe. "We all love you so much! We don't care how you look!"

"Hang the fucking bastards Katie!" Linda yelled. "Fucking pricks, hope they rot in bloody hell!"

Pulling Linda aside I told her the cops had 'accidently' beaten them up and they would make sure life in prison would be no picnic.

"Well that's fucking not enough!"

"Linda please watch your language, Lorna and Kyle are here." Mum's voice was stern, but soft. She knew how hurt, angry and worried my friends had been and how hard the ordeal had been for them.

"Whoops! I am sorry Mrs G. But it makes me so fucking cranky!"

"Linda, you need serious help with your Tourette's" said Nicole, bursting into uncontrollable laughter.

"Bullshit, I don't have fucking Tourette's you bloody fool! I just like fucking swearing."

Theresa entered the room; took one look at me and burst into tears.

"Oh Katie! Why you? This is so unfair!"

"It's ok Theresa. I am here and I'm alive. I will fight to the end to put those men away for a long time... and by the way Linda has Tourette's" that really cracked everyone up.

"Oh fuck off!" Linda replied just as Mum walked into the room and gave her a cake of soap.

"Sorry Mrs G, I am done now." Mum gave her a hug.

"You have Katie laughing so all is forgiven."

Theresa then went on to say Steven had come to the church dance looking for me last Friday.

"Oh?" I said.

"He was heartbroken when I said you were missing."

"Please tell me he doesn't know?" I asked.

"No, I haven't seen him since."

I snapped at them and made them promise to tell him I had a fight with Mum and ran away.

"Katie, talk to him." Nicole pleaded

"No! Don't be so fucking stupid. He's never going to be interested in me now, is he? Just bloody leave it alone okay?" God, I had forgotten about Steven! Damn, just when things were going alright I get sideswiped again. Was I ever going to be happy in my lifetime? Or was there always going to be another drama?

My barrister had asked for a closed court due to my age. But nothing was made easy for me. I was being attacked again and again by each of the barristers.

"You asked for it."

"You went willingly."

"You only cried rape when they refused to pay you." I had been violated in the worst possible way a woman can be and yet I was again the victim. This time it was by the courts. What right did the system have to treat me with such cruelty and contempt?

The second trial, like the first would be postponed. The first was because the defence needed more time. The second time supposedly a jury member had rung her own lawyer for advice. According to my barrister, it was all a ploy to buy the men more time. This was all over a period of three years. So I was forever reliving the horror over and over, all the evidence and the horrible smirks on those men who had not only hurt me, but had changed the way I would look at the world forever. The photos of my injuries; my torn bloodied clothes will always be in my brain. But throughout the whole ordeal, my little girl was always there. And when the courtroom became too much to handle I would be taken out to a room where my Mum and the rape crisis people were waiting.

I could feel the little girl close to me. Finally, it was over. The men were found guilty and the sentences ranged from five to fourteen years. The time they had already spent in jail was deducted from their sentence as they had not received bail over the three years. Me, I received a life sentence...

More nightmares followed and now a fear of the dark. The same dark I had once found such solace in. The case was over and the men were in prison. The police were happy, saying we had won. I certainly didn't feel like a winner... But I guess I was. I was alive and I had more strength than I had given myself credit for. A part of me died that dreadful night, but a part of me become stronger - I now knew I could face anything life threw at me, though I would forever be afraid to walk alone. For many years later, a car pulling up behind me would send me into a mad panic. A group of men walking near me would almost make my heart stop. For some reason I didn't die that night... So maybe my life did have purpose after all. Only time will tell...

Chapter 24

Katie

My nightmares are fewer. I see my Nanna's house. Its calm and I can see her at the window waiting for me. She is waving - I wave to her, but I can't go inside. It's like a force won't let me. I try to run but I'm stuck! Someone has a hold of me! I start to scream but nothing comes out. Then I hear the little girl.

"Wake up Katie. Wake up! It will be alright, just wake up!"

As I slowly open my eyes, I hear Kyle's giggles. "Get up sleepy head!"

I throw my pillow at him, yelling "Rack of hairy legs!"

"It's your birthday Katie!" He starts singing - "Happy birthday to you! Happy birthday to you! You look like a monkey and you smell like one too!" he's laughing at his own song.

"Well Kyle that makes you a monkey's brother!" I laughed, getting out of bed. Walking towards the kitchen, I hear Mum singing happily to herself.

"Good morning Katie! You look beautiful today. Happy eighteenth birthday, my darling!" She said as she walked close to hug me.

"Yay me! I can finally drink legally!" I laughed at my own joke.

"Oh; so not funny. Katie!" Mum replied, trying not to laugh.

Mum has been so happy lately. She had met a wonderful man. He was such a sweetheart. So loving and caring. He was good to us all, treating us kids like we were his own. Kyle loved him to pieces. He finally had the Dad he always wanted and needed.

"Katie, I have something to tell you" Mum said with a worried look on her face.

"Yes Mum? What is it?" I asked.

"Kenny asked me to marry him." She finally said, handing me a black ring box. I opened it and there was a huge diamond set in a white gold band.

"What did you say?" I asked her immediately. Getting over my shock - I was suddenly very excited for her.

"I told him I had to speak you, Kyle and Lorna first. And that I needed time to think." was her reply.

"Oh Mum! That's awesome! You so should! Yes!"

"Are you sure Katie?"

"Absolutely Mum... He is wonderful!" I reassured her.

"It's only been six months but I know I love him - I do know I want to grow old with him."

"Then say yes, you silly woman!" I said laughing at her.

"Okay, I will." She replied, suddenly jumping up and down screaming with excitement like a little girl.

"What the hell is all the bloody noise?" Kyle asks, walking into the kitchen.

"Munchkin! Quit the swearing!" I scolded.

"I will. Soon as someone tells me what all the bloody screaming is about!" He snapped back.

"Lorna! Come into the kitchen please. I have something to tell you and Kyle together." Mum yelled out.

"Kyle, Lorna - Kenny asked me to marry him." Mum told them both.

"Hell yes!" Kyle replied "Bloody hell yes!"

"Munchkin, my God... watch your language!" I reminded him, laughing at his excitement.

"Sorry Katie but that's damn good news" He replied. Lorna stood quietly not saying anything.

"Lorna, you okay? What do you think?" Mum asked in a worried voice.

"I'm happy for you Mum. I think that's great. I'm just sad today because my friend said she has to leave." Lorna answered in her usual manner.

"What friend sweetie?" Mum asked.

"Lorna, remember what I asked you?" I reminded her.

"It's okay Katie. I know Lorna sees people that we can't" Mum said.

"Why is she leaving?" Mum asked.

Stepping forward and placing her little fragile hands on Mums stomach, she replied. "Because of you..."

Turning a ghostly white, Mum asked. "Oh my... Lorna how did you know?"

"My friend told me." Lorna said.

"Know what?" I asked. Mum left the kitchen and returned with an old brown paper bag. She reached inside and took out an old pair of black boots. Lorna started to smile.

"Melinda said you wouldn't have forgotten her!" Mum started crying and fell to her knees, cradling the boots.

"Melinda, we were supposed to grow old together. Raise our children together" Mum said softly through her tears.

"She never left you Mum. She has always been here." Lorna reassured Mum as if she was the adult. Mum ran to her bedroom and came back almost in a hurry with an old black and white picture, handing the picture to Lorna.

"Yes Mum, that's Melinda." She said.

Looking at the picture, I said to Mum. "That's the little girl in my dreams!" I started to cry.

"That's Melinda and I, shortly before she died." Mum replied, holding back more tears.

"It was Melinda who saved me that night, from dying in the bag. It's her voice that wakes me up from my nightmares." I said, hardly believing what I was saying or witnessing. "She has helped me find the strength to go on."

"Yes, Melinda was a special person. My Earth Angel." Mum smiled.

Lorna stepped forward touching Mum's stomach again. "Melinda has to leave now."

"No!" I screamed. "Please don't leave me! How will I cope without you?"

Mum looked up and asks. "Why, Melinda? Why leave me now?"

Calmly Lorna replies "She has to. So she can return to you in seven months."

"What??? Lorna, you aren't making any sense!" I screamed.

"Oh my... Lorna! You know?" Mum asked.

"Yes Mum, I do. Melinda told me." She replied.

Mum said quietly "I didn't want to tell you all yet. But I'm having a baby. And I guess I'm having a girl." She was hugging the picture of her little friend.

"Katie, you will be alright now. You are a strong young woman with the world at your feet. Melinda is so proud of you, what you have become and what you have done."

"It's time to be an Earth Angel again and help people." Lorna said to mum's belly.

I was sitting on the floor, next to Mum, hugging tightly to Kyle. I never knew Melinda in her lifetime but now I know who she was. Mum's beloved friend... My Angel! A childhood promise to never leave Mum and to help sad people had been fulfilled. She was always there when I needed help and comfort. I could always feel her love and strength. All of a sudden, I feel her hand holding mine and something brushes across my face.

"Thank you." I whisper. "I will be alright." A light warm wind passes through the room.

"She's gone now." Lorna said softly. I was feeling more at peace with myself than I ever had. I looked down at Kyle.

"Are you crying Munchkin?"

"Don't be so bloody stupid Katie. It's the stupid cat's fur" He snapped.

"Awe, hairy legs...! You fibber, we don't have a cat" I teased. Helping Mum up off the floor I asked. "Don't you have a man to say yes too, Mum?"

I kissed Lorna softly on the cheek. "Thank you, Munchkin - for your wonderful gift. I have a feeling that our lives are going to be wonderful from this day forward."

Chapter 25

Felicity

The woman in the mirror wakes early today she has mixed feeling about the Flowers and the date with that Man. She is very sure she doesn't know him. So many things go through her mind but she has to see him for herself, be brave and face whatever lies ahead.

Going through her Wardrobe she finds something to wear. Choosing jeans a lovely white satin shirt with a brown floral scarf, brown high boots and grabbing a brown suit jacket. She sets about getting ready. Pulling her hair up in an orange flower clip she thinks maybe this is a stupid thing to do. Meeting a stranger but she reassures herself it was at Café, she was sure it would be full of people. To make sure she would be safe, she would catch a taxi there and back so she didn't have to walk to or from her car. Thinking things through a million times, changing her mind just as many. Checking her appearance in the mirror, she finally decides to go.

Getting very nervous as the taxi pulls up in front of the Café. Looking around she can't see anyone she recognizes, taking a deep breath she pays the taxi driver and books him to return in 2 hours. Climbing out of the taxi the woman in the mirror is confident but nowhere as confident as Felicity would be. The woman in the mirror is a survivor she has lived through enough to know what dangers are around.

Walking towards the Café door doesn't look like anyone is there, it appears to be empty as she opens the door she sees candles everywhere. Walking towards the counter where a Waitress is standing. All the sudden music fills the room its Queens's song "Love of my Life". She smiles she loves that song. Turning around the Man is standing there, looking straight at her. All the sudden the memories come flooding back like a movie theatre going off in her head, she now remembers him. How could she have ever forgotten him. About to burst into tears he steps forward.

"Dance with Me"

"Steven" she says

"I knew you would remember, you are still as beautiful as I remember Miss Katie" stepping forward to dance close to her.

"Ok. Not my fault if you end up with bruised feet and I must warn you I intend to step on your feet!"

"I'm so sorry" she whispered

He puts a finger on her lips

"I know Katie what happen I tried to find you for years but you shut me out. You were my 1st and only love... I have never forgotten you. I can't believe I have finally found you"

"This time Miss Katie I'm not letting you go" he whispered holding her very tightly.

All the sudden I was taken back to that night well over 30 years ago, he smelt so sweet. He was still so handsome, my sweet Knight. We chatted for hours about our lives, what happen and what path we had taken. Deciding to date taking things slowly as we now know we have all the time in the world. How lovely and thoughtful he still was...

How could I have forgotten him but with everything that happened in my life I choose to push things out of my mind, rather than deal with them. Was much easier to forget than face my fears. I was a survivor; I lived through so much horror. Though so many years have passed by I have never forgotten my nightmares, I learnt what caused of my nightmares, my emotions and my fears. I have learnt to deal with each situation as it happens, to be proud of who I am and what I have achieved no matter how big or small. Like the saying goes what doesn't kill you, you only make you stronger.

The woman in the mirror posting a Facebook status the next morning-"Isn't it just wonderful when you find an old school friend. All the sudden the awful school memories are faded and all the good memories come flooding back☺"

Today is my 49th Birthday; so excited, my family are all coming over.

"Get up Sleepy Head" I hear a man's voice.

Running to open the front door. I see My Munchkin. Kyle now in his early 40s still with that cheeky grin, and still as cute as a button. Kyle became a Rape Barrister and might I add one of the best in Australia. He couldn't help me that night, so he found a way to help as many women as he could. Married now He and his beautiful Wife have 3 sons... He is best Daddy any Child could wish for.

"Rack off Hairy legs "I said opening the door and running to hug him.

"I love you so much Munchkin"

"Love you More Miss Bossy Boots Katie" was his cheeky reply

So excited I see another car pull up. It's Lorna my sweet beautiful Lorna. Watching her walk up the driveway she is still a Gipsy, with long out of control black raven hair. Walking down the driveway with no shoes, clothes loose fitting and no sign of a bra. Still lost in her own world so typically Lorna. In her huge brown eyes I see so many souls. I just know she has been on this earth many times before. She chooses to use her gift to help people, that she does though her free web page. Also an establish author of 7 popular Children's Books. She is indeed one of a kind a special lady with a heart as big as the world.

Then Mum arrives, now in her early 70s. Still as beautiful as ever with her sweet 2nd husband our loving step Dad Kenny. They are still so much in love since the day they met, they are the perfect couple. I never saw mum wear dark glasses or long sleeves again. The day she met and then married Kenny she was never sad again. I swear her smile has gotten bigger over the years and you can tell Kenny adores her to pieces. He treats her like a Queen because she is worth it and she knows that now.

Then Mel our baby sister pulls up in her car with her Husband and 2 young daughters. Our Mel she is special to us. She gave us a final chapter in our lives, brought happiness when we had all been so sad. Named after Mum's childhood friend Melinda, my Little Girl. We just knew she was special with a wonderful old soul. Mel was very spoilt by Mum Kenny and us Older Kids. Seriously who cares that was our right, besides we were making sure this journey to earth, she would have everything and never be sad. She was so over protected, she was never alone...

With all my Family here celebrating my birthday I know I'm a lucky woman. Surrounded by so many people who love me, to have found Steven again. Maybe he is the love of my life, all I know is this time I'm going to give it a chance. I have been given a second chance is so many ways. I do have the odd nightmare but they don't scare me anymore. I always sleep with a light on but I'm not afraid. I haven't heard from my little Girl in a long time but I know she isn't far away from me; she will always be in my heart.

"Wake up Katie. Wake up! It will be alright, just wake up!" Oh yes I know I will be alright.

Lights Camera Action. Felicity enters the room as only she can the Song by Queen "Don't stop me now" the words summing her life up completely. She dances around to music so much has happened in her life, but she always manages to come back stronger. She is dressed as Wonder Woman. Gold headband around her Brown mid length wig, matching arm gold bands. A corset red top with gold laces her bootleg briefs are blue with white stars, a thick gold belt holding a gold rope. Her red knee high boots with gold laces, false eyelashes, trademark bright lips and nails complete her costume. She is Wonder woman done her way as only she can. She is Felicity she is confident she is a curvaceous middle aged woman, she is proud of her body and who she is.... No one can hurt her and nothing's going to stop her now...

She blows a kiss and waves goodbye....... This time the Cam zooms to a Yellow Teddy Bear, Black boots and Red stockings sitting in the corner of her room then shuts down................ ☺☺☺

♫*Tonight I'm gonna have myself a real good time*

I feel alive and the world it's turning inside out yeah!

I'm floating around in ecstasy

So don't stop me now don't stop me

'Cause I'm having a good time having a good time

I'm a shooting star leaping through the skies♫

♫*Like a tiger defying the laws of gravity*

I'm a racing car passing by like Lady Godiva

I'm gonna go go go

There's no stopping me

degrees♫

♫Don't stop me now I'm having such a good time

I'm having a ball don't stop me now

If you wanna have a good time just give me a call

Don't stop me now ('Cause I'm having a good time)

Don't stop me now (Yes I'm having a good time)

I don't want to stop at all♫

♫Don't stop me don't stop me don't stop me

Hey hey hey!

Don't stop me don't stop me♫

Ramblings of a Bipolar Mind.

My mind often wanders, always finding trouble focusing on the task and losing track of time. Simple things can become earth shattering as my brain scrambles the words into a mess. Some days you are on top of world other days you just want to hide not wanting to deal with any people, afraid they would find out your secrete and think you were crazy. Too tired, yet you sleep for hours, your brain working overtime never shutting off even to sleep. It can take forever before you're eventually fall asleep thinking, thinking, constantly- did I do that? Or who you upset, dwelling on the past always dragging it up never being able to let go.

Avoiding people you don't like or just avoiding conflict, paranoid of anyone and everything. Bipolar is a sickness yes, maybe you are born with it; maybe it was brought on through a tragic event. Unlike years ago, there wasn't much help for mental illnesses; you were considered a nutter, locked up in a padded room - shock treatments and poor understanding. Today we have readily available treatment, medications, therapy and support groups. You are never alone. If you were a diabetic you would take medication to stay alive wouldn't you? Don't be ashamed, be proud and love who you are...

Seek medical advice and join a support group if you have any signs of a mental illness. Seeking the right treatment can turn your Life around and put it back on track. Go speak to your Local Doctor in most cases Doctors are very understanding. Keep a diary of how you feel from day to day. Show it to your Doctor this can help them decide on right medication or treatment for you. Don't go through Life not happy or being sad... You are worth it, tell yourself that... Life is way too short for regrets. My Life is 100% better now I have come to terms with my Illnesses...

Signs of Bipolar and Depression.

BEHAVIOURS

Stopped going out

Not getting things done at work

Withdrawn from close family and friends

Relying on alcohol and sedatives

Stopped doing things you enjoy

Unable to concentrate

THOUGHTS

"I'm a failure"

"It's all my fault"

"Nothing good ever happens to me"

"I'm worthless"

"Life is not worth living"

FEELINGS

Overwhelmed

Unhappy, depressed

Irritable

Frustrated

No confidence

Guilty

Indecisive

Disappointed

Miserable

Sad

PHYSICAL

Tired all the time

Sick and run down

Headaches and muscle pains

Churning gut

Can't sleep

Poor appetite/weight loss.

These are facts taken from Beyond Blue Website.

Referencing belongs to Beyond Blue. For Help, support or someone to talk to. Please contact Beyond Blue Info line on 1300224636 or check out their website

http://www.beyondblue.org.au

Beyond Blue is an independent, not-for-profit organisation.

To make a donation - http://www.beyondblue.org.au

Email donations@beyondblue.org.au

Beyond Blue is truly a fantastic organisation.

What Puts a Person at Risk?

Around 2 per cent of people living in Australia will experience bipolar disorder at some stage of their lives. Bipolar disorder I is as common in men as it is in women, while Bipolar disorder II is twice as common in women as in men. Bipolar disorder can be influenced by a range of factors.

Bipolar Disorder I

People with this type of bipolar disorder are more likely to experience mania for longer periods of time and experience psychotic symptoms. Refer to signs and symptoms of bipolar disorder for more information.

Bipolar Disorder II

People with this type of bipolar disorder do not experience psychotic symptoms and generally have episodes of mania that last for a short time e.g. hours or at most, a few days. Also refer to signs and symptoms of bipolar disorder for more information.

In-between experiencing mania and depression, there are usually times when a person feels like they're on an even keel. However, if the person remains untreated, they are more likely to feel up and down more often.

Some people with bipolar disorder have what are called 'mixed episodes' where they feel some of the signs and symptoms of both depression and mania. Moods can change very quickly for some people - feeling high, then low and high again, within a matter of days or even hours.

People with bipolar disorder can also experience what is called 'rapid cycling'. This occurs when a person has at least four changes in mood states in any one year i.e. moving between depression, mania and a mixed episode.

Family history

Bipolar disorder seems to be most closely linked to family history. For example, while bipolar disorder affects around 2 per cent of the general population at some stage of their lives, people who have a parent with bipolar disorder have a 10 per cent chance of having the illness themselves.

<u>Environmental factors</u>

While a major cause of bipolar disorder seems to be genetic, stress can also trigger symptoms. Common triggers include:

•changing jobs

•changing living arrangements

•family and relationship problems

•being the victim of verbal, sexual, physical or emotional abuse or trauma

•other life transitions e.g. having a child

•death or loss of someone close.

Physical health issues

Physical health issues which can also trigger bipolar disorder include:

∘pregnancy and childbirth - refer to the postnatal depression section of this website.

∘hormonal problems (hyper and hypothyroidism)

∘brain problems (Parkinson's and Huntington's disease)

∘autoimmune problems (Lupus, HIV)

∘cancer (cancerous tumour and pancreatic cancer).

Helping Yourself

There are some basic steps people with bipolar disorder can take to manage their illness.

Postpone major life changes

Making major decisions and dealing with changes can be stressful at any time, but the situation can be worse if a person is unwell. A person with bipolar disorder should try to avoid major changes like moving house or changing jobs until they are feeling well.

Resolve personal conflicts

Stress in personal relationships is one of the most common triggers for bipolar disorder. Talking to a counsellor or psychologist can help a person find new ways to cope with problems.

Take part in enjoyable activities

Part of maintaining a balanced life means putting aside time to do enjoyable things such as exercising, meditating, reading, gardening or listening to music.

Keep work under control

Having too much work to do can create stress. Avoiding long hours and additional responsibilities and learning to say 'No' can help prevent work getting out of control.

Seek help

Talking to a friend, doctor, counsellor or someone else who is trusted, can help to relieve stress. Asking for help and support at home, work or in other activities can

Also reduce stress. Support groups provide an opportunity for people with bipolar disorder to discuss their common problems and find ways of dealing with them. There are also support groups for families and friends of people with bipolar disorder.

Practise breathing and muscle relaxation techniques

Stress can affect how a person breathes and can cause muscle tension. Breathing quickly and having tense muscles can, in turn, make a person feel more stressed. This vicious cycle can be stopped by learning and practising breathing and muscle relaxation techniques.

Eat a balanced diet

People who experience depression and mania may experience appetite changes. Even though a person with bipolar disorder may not feel like eating healthy foods when they are unwell, it's important that they try, even if it's only small snacks/meals. Drinking water to remain hydrated may also be helpful.

Establishing good sleeping patterns

Having a good night's sleep is important for maintaining good health. The body needs the opportunity to recharge from the day's activities.

If a person is in a manic phase, he/she may feel energetic and think they don't need much sleep. In fact, their bodies still need just as much sleep as usual.

Depression, however, can make people feel tired, but may also cause sleep disturbances like:

•difficulty getting to sleep

•not having a deep sleep

•waking very early in the morning and being unable to get back to sleep.

This can make symptoms of bipolar disorder worse e.g. irritability, tiredness and poor concentration. There are a number of things that can improve sleep patterns, including:-

In the morning...

The person should get out of bed as soon as they wake up. Don't go back to sleep or try to make up for lost sleep.

•Try to get up at a similar time each morning.

•Go outside into the fresh air.

•Do some physical activity e.g. go for a walk.

During the day...

•Don't nap before lunch or after dinner. Having a nap can make it hard to fall asleep at night.

•Deal with daily worries by setting aside some time for problem solving during the day.

•Keep a sleep-wake diary.

•Review sleep-wake patterns with a doctor at each visit.

•During the day, try to be physically active.

• Avoid drinking caffeine after 4pm and try not to drink more than two cups of caffeine-type drinks each day e.g. coffee, strong tea, cola or energy drinks.

Before going to bed...

•Avoid going to bed too early - it isn't the right time for deep sleep.

•Go to bed at a similar time each night.

•Avoid using alcohol to help fall asleep. When alcohol is broken down in the body, it causes people to sleep less deeply and to wake more frequently.

•Don't smoke within an hour or two of going to bed - it stimulates the nervous system.

•Don't go to bed hungry or with a full bladder.

•Allow time to wind down before going to bed - stop working, studying or exercising at least 30 minutes before bedtime.

•Use the bed only for sleep and sex so it becomes associated with sleep.

•Avoid taking sleeping pills for longer than a week - they can be addictive.

While you sleep...

•Make the bedroom quiet, dim and a comfortable temperature.

•Avoid too many blankets and electric blankets - being too hot makes it hard to get into a deep sleep.

Overcome long-term sleeping problems...

1. Get up if unable to sleep after trying for 15 to 20 minutes.

2. Do something to take your mind off trying to get to sleep e.g. play cards, read, knit enjoy a warm bath, do a crossword or watch TV.

3. Go back to bed when more relaxed and sleepy.

4. If still awake after a further 15 to 20 minutes, get out of bed and try the routine again.

Keep active

Exercise is important for maintaining both good physical health and mental health.

Some tips for keeping active

Plan - A person with bipolar disorder should make a plan, so they participate in some enjoyable activities every day and finish each day with a sense of achievement.

Start small and build up slowly - If a person is going through a period of depression, they may have difficulty with simple things such as getting up and getting dressed in the morning. Don't try to do too much too early. It's a good idea to start with easy activities and slowly build on them.

Include other people - When people don't feel like doing much, planning social outings/activities can help them get moving. If the person doesn't have an established social network, they could consider joining a local club or group.

Don't be too hard on yourself - A plan is only a rough guide that should be flexible. If an activity runs overtime or can't be completed, skip it and move onto the next one.

Reward yourself - Allow time to do enjoyable, interesting, relaxing and satisfying activities. Some cheap, entertaining and easy pass-times include reading, listening to music, watching movies, gardening, going to the beach or park, taking part in sporting or creative activities, shopping, seeing friends and playing with pets.

Exercise physiologists are people who have an understanding of how exercising affects the body and mind. They can help people get motivated, develop an individual exercise plan and stay on track.

Reducing alcohol and other drugs

•Many people treat their mood problems by drinking alcohol, smoking tobacco and cannabis and taking other drugs.

•Although these substances may provide temporary relief, they can cause long-term problems.

•Most illegal drugs and alcohol interfere with the effects of medication. If a person has been consuming large amounts of alcohol or other drugs, it's important to tell the doctor, so an appropriate treatment plan can be worked out.

•People often find it difficult to stop cigarette smoking and may need to seek advice from a health professional.